Good Cookies

SENI MARQUIS

CHAPTERS

CHAPTER 1...2

CHAPTER 2 16

CHAPTER 3 46

CHAPTER 4 74

CHAPTER 5 90

CHAPTER 6 108

CHAPTER 7 123

CHAPTER 8 143

CHAPTER 9 156

CHAPTER 10 169

CHAPTER 11 179

CHAPTER 12 199

CHAPTER 13..214

CHAPTER 14 228

CHAPTER 15.. 238

CHAPTER 1

"Cookie, you feel so good... I can't take it!"

"Hold on Tony, don't cum yet."

"I can't hold it. Ohh I'm coming! Sorry... Girl, you got the best cookies in the world. Oreos ain't got nothing on you," Tony said, panting, trying to catch his breath.

Cookie didn't reply. She just got up and walked over to her dresser. She opened the bottom drawer and pulled out a small bullet shaped vibrator.

"What is that?" Tony asked, with a puzzled look.

"It's called a 'magic bullet'."

"And what is it for? I hope you don't think you are sticking that thing in my back door, 'cause this ain't that type of party."

"Don't worry, it's for me, not you," Cookie replied smugly.

"For what?" he asked.

"To finish the job."

"Don't worry baby, give me a couple minutes to get myself together and I got you. You don't need no 'magic bullet'."

Cookie rolled her eyes and sat in her special 'fun chair'.
The fun chair was located in the corner of her room, right in front of the mirror. It was a soft, flexible chair that she had bought from a novelty sex store, made just for situations like this. She placed both feet on the foot rest and opened her legs. She guided the bullet inside of her, and let out a soft moan. She began to breath heavy as she pulled it out to vibrate against her clit.

Tony looked on in amazement. It turned him on to watch her pleasure herself. He walked towards her, as he stroked himself. He stood directly in front of her, trying to get her attention, but her eyes were closed. She was lost in her own world. Tony got on his knees and started to kiss her inner thigh, but she quickly pushed him away. Tony, being the persistent person he was, smiled, leaned in again and put one of her 36Cs in his mouth.

Cookie was in ecstasy with the feeling of his warm mouth on her nipple, along with the little bullet driving her toward an orgasm. Her soft moans turned into loud screams as the juices started to trickle from her dripping wet center. She dropped the bullet on the floor and continued to breathe heavily.

Tony took that as an invitation for another round. He stood up and tried to enter her again but she quickly forced her legs closed.

"Come on baby. I'm as hard as a rock right now. Let me get another sample of that sweet cookie," Tony begged.

"Sorry, but it's not gonna happen. You got yours and I got mine. Besides, it's getting late. Ain't it about time you get home to your wife and kids?"

"Come on now... Why you gotta be like that? I told you my wife and I are separated. We just live together for the sake of the children. We don't even sleep in the same room. She does her thing and I do mine."

"Yeah... Okay... It don't matter because--"

"But it does matter, Cookie," he said, cutting her off mid-sentence. "We've been seeing each other for close to a year now, and I am really feeling you. Just give me some time to handle my situation at home and then we can be together."

"Whatever you say. Look, I'm tired. I'm gonna take a shower and then go to sleep."

"Well, can I join you?" he asked.

"No Tony. I'll call you tomorrow," Cookie said as she walked into the bathroom, closing the door behind her.

"Okay... Do you need any money before I leave?" he asked.

"What do you think, Tony?" she yelled through the door.

*   *   *

The next day, Cookie strolled into work and went straight to the teacher's lounge. After graduating from college with an Associate's Degree in Early Childhood Education, she had found a job teaching first grade math. Everyone on the staff knew she was sleeping with the principal, Tony Harris, even though she had tried to be discreet. Tony was openly affectionate towards her, despite her objections.

While drinking a cup of coffee, her best friend Carol walked in.

"Girl, you look like you had a rough night," she said cheerfully.

"Hey Carol, I did have a rough night," Cookie replied.

"Well, we have about ten minutes before the little rug rats show up, so go ahead and spill the beans." There were a few other teachers in the lounge, so Cookie scooted her chair closer to Carol.

"Last night, Tony was at my house and he didn't want to leave. He kept telling me how much he loves me and how he's about to divorce his wife so we can be together," Cookie whispered.

"I don't know what you do to these men but you have them all going crazy over you."

"I'll tell you what it is. It's the sex. They can't get enough of my sweet, chocolate chip, sugar cookies," she said, laughing. Her laughter stopped short when Tony walked into the lounge.

"Good morning, everyone," he said to the room with a smile.

One by one, the teachers slowly began to leave the lounge to head to their classrooms. Tony wasn't a bad principal, he was just a no-nonsense type of guy. He was often very critical and rarely had anything nice to say. However, Cookie was another story. He never stopped complimenting her.

"Good morning, Mr. Harris," Cookie said as she stood and headed for the door.

"I thought I told you to drop all that 'Mr. Harris' crap. Besides, last night you called me, Tony. You said my name quite a few times if I'm not mistaken," he said, pulling her in for a hug.

"And I thought, I told you to give me some space when we're at work? It doesn't set a good example for the kids to see us fraternizing." Cookie replied as she backed away.

She gathered her belongings and headed for the door. On her way out Tony gave her a little slap on her backside. She shot him a menacing glare and kept going.

*　　*　　*

Cookie stayed at her desk after school to grade some papers. A few minutes after she started, Carol walked in her classroom.

"Hey, Miss Thang, how were the rug rats today?"

"First of all, Carol, my kids are not rug rats and they were fine: except for that Tommy Mitchell. He bullies almost all of his classmates. I'm going to talk to his parents at the upcoming parent-teacher conference."

"I already know about little Tommy Mitchell. Last week he made another little boy fall and hurt himself. When he came to the nurse's office, he was so afraid to say who had done it that he wet himself. I had to hear it from another boy."

"Well, I hope after I talk to his parents, they will straighten him out," Cookie said.

"I doubt it. In most cases, the bully gets bullied at home, so they return the favor at school or somewhere else," Carol responded.

"Anyway, enough about that. What's good for tonight? It's Friday night, we just got paid and I want to get my groove on," Cookie said as she did a little dance.

"I thought you'd never ask! My man is out of town and there is a new club called the Hot Spot that I've been wanting to check out," Carol said with a grin.

"Then, the Hot Spot it is. I do have to go to the bank first, then get my nails done and call my cousin to do something with my hair. I'll meet you at your place at eleven..?"

"No, Cookie. I'll come to your house because you are always late and the Hot Spot will be jumping by then. We need to get there as early as possible," Carol said.

"Okay, come to my house and I'll ride with you in that brand new car of yours," Cookie paused. "On second thought, I'll follow you, just in case I meet someone." Cookie winked conspiratorially.

"Girl please, what about Tony? You know he ain't having that," Carol said, laughing.

"Having what? Did you forget that he has a wife and kids? I'm free to share my cookies with anyone I choose." Before Carol could respond, Tony walked into the classroom.

"Speak of the devil," Carol whispered under her breath.

"Hey Cookie," Tony said, kissing her on the cheek.

"Hi Tony, but I'm not the only one in here," she replied.

"Oh... Yeah... Hi Carol," Tony added dryly.

"Don't do me any favors by speaking to me," Carol said with attitude.

"See..? That's why I didn't say anything in the first place," he said.

"Come on, guys, please don't start," Cookie pleaded.

Neither one responded to her plea. Tony looked at Cookie and said,

"Anyway, I just swung by to see if we can hook up tonight. I was thinking maybe dinner and a movie. Or we can skip them both and go skinny dipping in my pool. My wife and kids went away for the weekend so I have the house all to myself."

"Who wants to go skinny dipping with your old, flabby ass?" muttered Carol to Cookie, a little louder than she meant to. Cookie burst out laughing as Tony shot them both a look that would scare most people.

"I'm sorry Tony, but the two of us already have plans for tonight."

"Oh, where are y'all going?" he asked.

"None of your business, because your old ass is not invited," Carol retorted.

"Look, I'm tired of your mouth, you weave wearing heifer! I'll go anywhere I please. I don't need an invitation!" he yelled.

"Calm down baby, please?" Cookie asked, rubbing his chest. "We're going to this new club called the Hot Spot. It's a girls night out sort of thing, but, if you're still up when we leave, I'll come over to your place for a little midnight snack."

"You promise?" he asked.

"Yeah, I promise," she replied. He nodded in agreeance.

"Okay. You know I got a sweet tooth and I need a bite of that cookie."

"Don't worry, I got you," she answered. Tony gave her a quick peck on the lips and left.

Carol rolled her eyes when he closed the door. "I don't know what you see in him," she said.

"Please, Carol, don't start. Let's just concentrate on having a good time tonight," Cookie begged.

"Whatever you say, girl. I'll call you when I'm on my way to your house."

"Okay, but first tell me what kind of place is this Hot Spot? What should I wear? Something more formal, casual, or slutty?" she asked, giggling.

"I don't know. I guess it depends on what you're going for. If you plan to sit at the bar all night and get your drink on, go more formal. If you're going to get your dance on, go with something more casual and comfortable. But, if you're looking to catch a man for a one night stand, then I'd say the slutty look is the way to go," Carol said, laughing.

"Girl, you crazy. Call me when you're on your way."

CHAPTER 2

Cookie was running a little late trying to get to the bank. She had stayed at school longer than she intended and it was nearly closing time. She pulled into the parking lot and ran inside the bank. It seemed like she wasn't the only one trying to cash her check at the last minute, because the line for the teller was long. She was the last person in line and when it finally came to her turn the teller gave her attitude because it had been a long day and she wanted to get home.

"Hello," Cookie said, smiling pleasantly.

"Yeah? What can I do for you?" The teller responded, rudely.

"I would like to deposit my check."

"Okay, well can we hurry this up? You're my last customer today and I want to get out of here," said the teller.

"Excuse me? I don't know what your problem is, but I've had a long day too. All I want to do is cash my check, deposit some of it into my account and take my ass home! Now, I suggest you just do your job before it gets ugly in here!" Cookie yelled, pointing her finger in the teller's face. The bank manager heard the commotion and came out of his office to see what was going on.

"Donna, what seems to be the problem here?" he asked the teller.

"There's no problem, Mr. Robinson," Donna replied.

"Actually sir, there is a problem. This ignorant lady is being very rude and disrespectful. All I wanted to do is deposit my check and go about my business," said Cookie.

For the first time since he came out of his office, he turned to look at the disgruntled customer. His heart skipped a beat as he looked into her eyes. She was an angel.

"Oh. I'm sorry for any inconvenience ma'am; please, let me take care of this matter personally for you." He waved a hand absently at the disgruntled teller to dismiss her, not breaking eye contact with Cookie. "Donna, I'll handle Miss----?"

"Taylor," Cookie replied.

"Yes. I'll handle Miss Taylor. Donna, you can go ahead and cash out. I've got it from here."

"Okay Mr. Robinson," Donna said as she rolled her eyes. The bank manager didn't seem to notice and Cookie let this act of defiance slide.

"Miss Taylor, would you follow me to my office please?" he asked.

Entering his office, Cookie looked around. It was nicely decorated with African art and pictures of his kids. As she sat down, she read his name plate.

Eugene Robinson. She also noticed a wedding photo of him with his wife.

"Do you have your ID Miss Taylor?" he asked with a smile. Cookie looked through her purse but couldn't find her license.

"I'm sorry, I think I left it in my desk at work," Eugene nodded and glanced down at her paycheck.

"So you're a teacher at MLK elementary?" he asked.

"Yes. A math teacher," she said shyly. Eugene smiled,

"Both of my kids go there. I sure wish I had a teacher that looked as good as you do when I was young. I probably would have done better in school."

"Oh, I don't know... It looks to me that you turned out alright," she said, blushing slightly.

"Yeah, but imagine if my math teacher was as sexy as you? I would probably own the bank instead of just being the manager," he teased, laughing. Cookie laughed as well, blushing even more. After a little more flirting, Eugene deposited her check and walked her to her car. She wanted to ask him for his number but waited for him to make the first move.

Eugene wanted to ask her for her number but he and his wife had just gotten back together after he was caught having an affair. He didn't want to risk ruining all the progress he'd made in his marriage. So, they shook hands as they stared into each other's eyes and then went their separate ways.

*　　*　　*

As she drove towards the nail salon, Cookie couldn't help thinking about the obvious attraction between them. Eugene looked to be about 6'2", around 220 pounds with brown skin with hazel eyes. He had a low hair cut with deep waves and a dimple in his cheek on the left side. Cookie knew he was married. Part of her didn't care and another part said to stay far away from him. She quickly got her nails done even though it was crowded. She was a salon regular, so they bumped her ahead of some other waiting customers when she walked in.

Since she needed her hair done and her cousin didn't answer her phone, she went to Unique's Hair and Spa treatment. The place was packed. It seemed like everyone wanted to get their hair done at the same time. It was Friday night after all.

"Hey, Cookie," said Unique, owner and first chair stylist.

"What's up, 'Nique? I see it's jumping in here."
"Yeah girl... You know how it is on Friday's. Everybody and their mama's trying to look good for the weekend."

"I know that's right. How many more heads you got 'til you can hook mine up?" Cookie asked.

"Girl, I'm booked for the rest of the night, but I can see if the new girl, Sabria, can squeeze you in," she replied.

After about two hours of waiting and gossiping, Cookie was finally able to get her hair done. Happy with the results, Cookie gave Sabria a nice tip and headed home.

*   *   *

After showering and getting dressed, Cookie checked herself out in her full length mirror, liking what she saw.

Since she had a black father and white mother, Cookie had the best of both worlds. She got her long straight hair and light gray eyes from her mother's side and her smooth skin and thick curves from her father's side. Cookie, whose actual name was Natasha Taylor, was built, as they say, like a brick house. At 5'5", she had the body of a video vixen and the face of an angel. Many people compared her to a lighter skinned Stacy Dash.

With her black and silver strapless Prada dress and silver Jimmy Choo's, she knew she would kill them at the club and she started walking down the stairs to get a light snack before she started drinking for the night. She glanced in the mirror as she passed it in the hall, thinking, *darn, I look good! But something's missing.* She noticed the black Prada shades on the table and realized that was the finishing touch.

Cookie began fixing herself a turkey and cheese sandwich and her thoughts drifted to Mr. Eugene Robinson. *That man is fine,* she thought. *But he's got a wife and kids and I just can't deal with another married man.*

Her thoughts were interrupted by the sound of the doorbell. She took a bite of her sandwich as she walked to the door.

She opened it without first checking who it was, thinking it was Carol. She started to choke on her food when she realized it was her ex-boyfriend, Sam. Well, Psycho Sam, as everyone called him, and for good reason.

"Hey baby. What, you get choked up when you see me? I didn't know I still had that effect on you," Sam said, with a sinister grin.

Cookie was lost for words as she looked at a man she thought was out of her life. She stuttered,

"S-S-Sam. What are you y-y-you doing here?"

"You don't sound happy to see me," he replied. Cookie didn't respond, she was speechless, and not just from the sandwich she was choking on. Sam shrugged and continued.

"Anyway, you're looking really good, baby. What, you got a hot date?" Sam asked, walking past her into the house as if he owned it.

"Yes, I'm going out, and I don't think it's wise for you to be here," Cookie said, nervously.

"I wrote you a thousand letters while I was in prison, but you never wrote back. I was hurt by that. But it's Okay... I forgive you and I'm willing to leave that in the past and move on with our lives," he said as he grabbed her and began to caress her body.

Cookie was frozen stiff and scared out of her mind. Sam was called "Psycho" for a reason. He was totally crazy. Cookie knew she had to do her best not to set him off. Just as Sam was leaning in for a kiss, Carol walked in.

"Hey, Cookie, why is your front door wide open... Oh, I'm sorry. I didn't know you had company," she said. As Sam turned around and Carol realized who he was, she knew there was going to be trouble if the two of them didn't get out of there fast.

"Hey Carol. I see you two are still as thick as thieves," Sam sneered.

"Hi Sam...Cookie, are you ready to go?"

"Yes, I am. Just let me grab my purse," replied Cookie.
"Where do you think you're going? I came all the way over here and you're just going to leave? I don't think so," he said, grabbing her arm.

"Let go of me, Sam. You're hurting my arm!" Cookie yelped.

"Shut up! I have been locked up for a long five years and we have a lot of catching up to do," he said, holding her in place. Carol had her cell phone in her hand and quickly dialed 911.

"Yes, I'm at my friend's house and her ex-boyfriend just showed up. He already grabbed her and won't let her go. Can you send someone out here to help?" Carol said frantically.

"Oh, it's like that? I see some things never change," Sam said, pushing his way past Carol and out the door. "Don't worry, I'll see you again. And next time? You'll be singing another tune!" he yelled over his shoulder.

"Cookie, are you alright?" Carol asked. Cookie nodded weakly.
"Yeah. Thanks for calling the police. That was a real heads up move."

"It's all good, but I didn't really call the cops. I just wanted him out of here," Carol said, smiling.

"What? Girl, you are crazy!" Cookie told her.

"No, Psycho Sam is the crazy one. Now let's get out of here before he realizes I didn't actually call the cops and decides to come back," Carol suggested.

"I really don't feel like going out now. He ruined my mood," said Cookie.

"Now you're the crazy one! You can't let that man have you living in fear. So go get your purse and let's be out!"

It took a little more convincing, but Cookie finally gave in and followed Carol to Hot Spot. As soon as they got through the door, Carol jumped into the crowd to dance. It took Cookie a while longer to get settled in and relax, since she still had Sam on her mind, but she eventually got into the swing of things. After a few drinks, she decided to join Carol on the dance floor.

Carol had a drink in her hand and was dancing with two guys, having a great time. But it seemed like time stopped and everyone turned to look at Cookie when she stepped onto the dance floor. Even the guys with Carol slowed down to stare at Cookie. She noticed all eyes on her.

"Shout out to the honey in the black and silver dress!" shouted the DJ. "This song goes out to you, sexy!"

He played the popular club banger, 'Pretty girls in the V.I.P.' by the local artist D-Rocca.

With a drink in one hand and her purse in the other, Cookie started slowly rotating her hips to the music. The guys were staring and drooling over her as if she was a T-bone steak and they were hungry dogs. When Carol heard the DJ's shout out to Cookie, she made her way over to where she was dancing by herself.

"Hey girl, this is my jam right here!" Carol shouted over the music as she started to dance provocatively with her friend.

"Girl, everyone is staring at us!" Cookie said laughing but she decided to join in the dance with Carol.

Towards the end of the song, one brave guy, determined to join the two fine females as they danced, tried his luck and slid in behind Cookie.

His friend stepped in front of Carol. They smiled and began to include them in their sexy dance. The DJ switched to some reggae, which Carol and Cookie really got into. A few songs later, they headed to the bar to refill their drinks.

"I'll have a Grey Goose and cranberry and my girl will have a Sex on the Beach," Cookie said, flashing a smile at the bartender.

"This place is really nice. We should come here more often," Carol observed.

"Yeah, the bartender is a cutie too," Cookie replied.

"I'm glad we came here," said Carol, smiling. The bartender went to hand them their drinks, but before Cookie could pay for them, someone slapped a fifty dollar bill on the bar.

"Their drinks are on me and you can get me a double shot of Patron," Tony said with a smile. Cookie turned around and saw that it was Tony. Carol ground her teeth at the sight of him, grabbed her drink and headed back to the dance floor.

"Hey, Tony. What are you doing here?" Cookie asked.

"What? A white guy can't come to this club?" he asked, teasingly.

"Boy, you silly! I'm just surprised to see you here."

"Well, me and a couple of friends decided to have a guys' night out of our own."

"Yeah, whatever. Let's go dance and see if white men are as stiff as they say," Cookie said, grabbing his hand.

"Come on then. I'll show you that white men got a little bit of rhythm. I hope you can keep up," he joked.

"We'll see," Cookie replied. Deep down, she was glad to see Tony because she really didn't want to go back to her house in case Sam showed up. Tony didn't know it, but his presence made her feel safer.

On the dance floor, Cookie ground against him like a stripper would. He couldn't contain himself, nor could he hide the growing erection in his pants. Cookie noticed, and ground against him harder. The crowd looked on in amazement while the white guy, who looked totally out of place, danced for three straight songs with the hottest girl in the club.

At the end of the night, the girls said goodnight and went their separate ways. Carol drove away with a mystery man she had met that night. Cookie made a mental note to get the details from her the next day.

Cookie and Tony went to get a bite to eat at an all-night diner.

"So, what happened to your friends?" Cookie asked after the waiter brought their drink orders.

"Well, the truth is I came alone," he admitted.

"I kinda figured that," she said, smiling. He at least had the decency to look sheepish.

"But, I wanted to see you. Might I add you look good enough to eat?" he said, with a wink.

"Well, why couldn't you wait until I left the club? I told you I would call you and come over?" she asked.

"I was going to wait, but then, my wife came home early. She was talking about leaving the kids at her parents so she and

I could rekindle the flames in our marriage," he said.

"What's wrong with that? She's just trying to make it work. You should give it a chance," Cookie told him.

"Whatever. We had plenty of chances and the love is just not there anymore. So, that's why I left and went to the club. Besides, I didn't want some young thug eating my cookies," he said, smiling as he reached for her hand.

The waiter brought out their food and they ate in silence for a few minutes.

"What's on your mind, Cookie?" he asked.

"I'm just trying to figure out where this is going."

"What do you mean?" Tony asked, looking confused.

"I mean us. I'm 26, single, with no kids and you're 45 and married with two teenagers and a 20 year old. Not to mention you're white. There's a damn near 20 year age difference between us," she pointed out.

"For one thing, age ain't nothing but a number, and second, since when did being white have anything to do with it? You *are* half white, if you haven't forgotten! And I told you, me and my wife are separated. We're staying together for appearances' sake until my two youngest finish high school."

"Tony, they are both only 14 and freshmen in high school! You expect me to wait around another three years for you, when we've already been seeing each other for almost a year?" she asked.

"I'm not asking for anything more than what we already have. I can't deny that I love you and I understand that my situation is hard to deal with. So let's just ride it 'til the wheels fall off. I know you could meet someone special any day but until then, just let me have my cookies and milk," he stated.

"Okay, as long as we're on the same page. I'm not trying to lead you on. It is what it is until it's over," she said.

"Whatever you say, honey. It's your world, baby. I'm just a kid trying to get a cookie," Tony said with a devilish smile.

*   *   *

After eating, they stood around in the parking lot for a little while, trying to figure out their next move. Tony wanted to go with Cookie, but she didn't want to go back to her house.

"Why can't we go to your place?" she asked.

"I told you, that my wife came back early, so we can't go there. Why don't you want to go back to your house like we normally do?" Tony asked, noticing tears building up in Cookies eyes. He pulled her close and whispered in her ear, "what's the matter, baby? Talk to me."

She broke down and told him everything about Psycho Sam and how after five years in prison, he had showed up at her house, making demands and threatening her.

"It was a good thing Carol was there or there's no telling what he would have done to me!" she cried.

"Don't worry, Cookie, I got you. I won't let him hurt you," Tony said, hugging her tight.
He followed Cookie to her house and decided to stay with her until she fell asleep. He'd go home after he knew she was safe. He had told his wife, he was going over to a friend's house to watch the game. He hoped she would be sleeping by the time he got home.

Damn, I hope this Psycho Sam guy isn't as crazy she made him sound. I mean, she's got some good cookies, but it ain't worth dying for, he thought to himself as he followed behind her maroon Camry.

Cookie was lost in her own thoughts as she drove back to her house.

I really hope that Sam doesn't come back. I just want him to leave me alone. And I have no idea what Tony's old bones will do if he does show up. But, I would rather have him with me than be at the house alone.

When they finally arrived at Cookie's home, they went straight upstairs. Cookie hopped in the shower while Tony watched TV. Even though he wanted to have sex with her, he was nervous because he'd had sex with his wife before he went to the club and hadn't washed up afterwards. Since he didn't want her to notice the smell of sex on him, he decided to join her in the shower.

Cookie was humming one of the songs she had heard that night when Tony crept into the shower. At the sight of her body, covered in soap suds, he became aroused. Tony grabbed one of her sponges and lathered it with soap. She smiled as she looked down and noticed his manhood getting larger. She thought he was pretty well hung, for a white guy. Cookie turned around and he started using the sponge on her back. He slowly and gently scrubbed the back of her neck and worked his way down to her round bottom. She giggled, amazed at the way the soap felt as it found her very special spot.

He put the sponge down and turned her to face him. He got down on one knee and dove in face first into her forbidden fruit while she grabbed the back of his neck and the water from the shower poured down his face. He felt like he was drowning, but the soft moans she was making fueled him to keep going. He started to get a cramp in his leg, so he stood and scooped Cookie up along with him. Tony was strong and in good shape, but she was afraid that he might drop her.

Once he slid himself inside her, she forgot her fear. Cookie wrapped her arms around his neck while licking his ear lobe. That little motion made him thrust deeper inside her. She took things into her own hands and bounced up and down on his shaft.

"Damn, Cookie, you are so tight! I love you, baby." Tony grunted.

"You don't love me, you just love my cookies," she replied, bouncing so hard he felt like he might drop her. Tony placed her down on the floor and she spun around, with her back facing him, so he could penetrate her from behind. Cookie gasped as entered her quickly.

"Slow down, baby. I don't want you to come yet," she said.

"Don't worry. I'm not coming yet. I'm gonna be at this all night... Oh, oh I'm sorry, baby, but I gotta let it go! You're so warm and soft, I can't help it!" Tony moaned. Cookie reached down and began to massage her clit. While she pleasured herself with one hand, she used the other to push off the wall and throw herself onto Tony's manhood with more force. He started to shake and exploded inside of her. She continued to grind against him until he became soft.

Afterwards, they got back into the shower and then dried each other off. Cookie wasn't satisfied, so she sat on the edge of the tub and pulled Tony towards her. As she looked up at him, she slowly took him into her mouth until his eyes rolled back into his head. She continued until he was hard again. She stood up and bent over with her hands on the edge of the tub.

He entered her from behind again, but this time Cookie was determined to get off. She started throwing it back into him so hard that she was pushing Tony backwards with each thrust. He planted his feet and pushed back, matching her stroke for stroke. He was pounding into her harder and harder, as he got more and more into it. He slapped her ass, leaving a light red hand print.

Tony pulled on her hair, and when she screamed for more, he pumped as hard as he could. Unfortunately, this caused her to lose her balance and fall forward into the tub. He lost his footing as well, and fell in with her. They both burst out laughing and decided to move to the bedroom.

After a passionate 45 minutes of rough sex, Cookie passed out with the hint of a smile on her lips.

Tony knew he was going to be in trouble with his wife, so he gathered his things and got ready to leave. When he opened the front door and saw his car, he couldn't believe his eyes. His brand new Dodge Durango looked like it had been through a war. All four tires were slashed and the windshield and side windows were shattered. To top it off, the letters "P.S." were carved into the hood, roof and passenger side door of the SUV.

"What the hell?!" Tony yelled loudly. As he was still in the doorway of Cookie's house, she woke up and ran down the stairs to see what was wrong.

"What's the matter with..." she asked, cutting herself off when she noticed Tony's car. Once she saw the huge "P.S." carved into the hood, she knew exactly who was behind it. Psycho Sam.

He must have been waiting near the house and saw us go inside together, she thought to herself.

"Who in the world would do such a thing?" Tony said, examining the damage, as he looked back at Cookie.

"Do you know who did this?" he asked. Cookie didn't answer him. She was busy looking around for any signs of Sam. Tony kept calling her name and when she didn't respond the third time, he grabbed her by the shoulders and shook her.

"Cookie, what's wrong with you? Didn't you hear me calling your name?" he asked insistently.

"I'm sorry," she said, eyes downcast.

"Do you have any idea who could have done this?" he asked again.

"Sam," she whispered, so low that he couldn't hear her.

"What did you say? Speak up!"

"I said Sam!" she yelled. "The 'P.S.' stands for Psycho Sam. It was him."

"I can't believe this shit! You let your crazy ex-boyfriend ruin my brand new car?" he asked, amazed.

"First of all, I didn't **let** him do anything. I told you how crazy he was but I never thought he would do anything like this."

Shortly after Tony dialed 911, the police arrived and he filled out a report with the attending officer. He took pictures with the camera on his phone and called a tow truck to take his car to an auto shop. "Are you going to stay here or do you want me to give you a ride home?" Cookie asked with obvious concern.

"I don't want anything from you. You've already done enough," he replied sarcastically. "Besides, there's a cab already on the way to come get me."

Once the police left and his car had been towed away, he jumped into the cab and left without saying goodbye. He didn't even look her way.

CHAPTER 3

On Monday, when Cookie went back to work, she tried to speak to Tony, but he completely ignored her. The same happened on Tuesday, Wednesday and Thursday. On Friday when she went to the office to pick up her paycheck, she decided enough was enough. Cookie marched into his office.

"Tony, we need to talk," she demanded.

"How can I help you, Miss Taylor?" he asked.

"Oh, now I'm Miss Taylor?" she asked. Tony looked up from his paper work and had to fight the urge to jump up and kiss her.

Truth be told, he wasn't mad at her, he was just nervous to be around her again because of Psycho Sam and his reputation for violence and irrational behavior. He could smell her perfume and he got hard just looking at her in her Vera Wang dress. He knew that seeing her again could lead to trouble, but the way his body reacted to her whenever he saw her made him go against his better judgment.

"What's going on, Cookie?" he asked, softening up towards her.

"That's what I want to know," she responded.

"It's not you. It's that Psycho Sam character. He worries me and I felt like I should give you some space."

"Well, if that's what you want, then fine, but I am truly sorry for what he did to your car. I'm willing to pay for all the damages," she said.

"Thank you, but no need. My insurance company is taking care of it." He looked at her and decided he couldn't stay mad at her any longer. "Anyway, how have you been? I've really missed you," he said, sincerely.

"Oh, yeah, I could tell. You have been giving me the cold shoulder all week," Cookie replied.

"I know, and I apologize. Let me make it up to you," he said.

"I thought you wanted some space," she said.

"We've had enough space between us this week. Besides, you know I've got a sweet tooth and I really need me some of those cookies," Tony said, with a flirtatious smile.

"When do you want to hook up?" she asked.

"How about I come to your house tonight?" he asked.

"Nah, I'm chilling with Carol tonight. And I want you to take me out first. Maybe a movie and then dinner. Afterwards, we can go to my place for dessert," she said, smiling.

"OKAY, it's a date. Let's make it for Sunday."

"Can't wait," Cookie said, giving Tony a hug and a kiss on the cheek before leaving his office.

*　　*　　*

On the way to the bank to deposit her check, Cookie's mind was all over the place. She thought about Tony. She knew she didn't love him, but she did care for him and didn't want to see him get hurt. She also thought about Sam. He had shown up at her house with flowers and jewelry a couple of nights earlier.

The jewelry was probably stolen, she thought to herself.

At one point in time, she had been deeply in love with Sam, but he was very jealous and possessive. He had never physically abused her, but he had done so mentally and verbally. When he went to jail, she had finally felt free and vowed to never be in that kind of relationship again. Sam was hot or cold, there was no happy medium.

When he came to her house he tried really hard to charm her and tried everything he could think of to get her back. When she refused, he got upset and threatened her. Cookie told him, that she would call the police and that was the only reason he left, but that didn't stop him from trying again day after day. He was very persistent.

Cookie pulled into the bank parking lot. She looked in the rear view mirror and reapplied another coat of lip gloss and sprayed a little bit of perfume on her dress. She laughed to herself, at how far she would go to impress another married man.

*   *   *

Eugene had put on his best suit, hoping that Miss Taylor would show up to cash her check. He'd been thinking about her all week, going so far as fantasizing about her while he made love to his wife. There were only about 30 minutes left until closing time and he was out front hoping she would walk in before then. His prayers were answered as Cookie made her way into the bank doors.

They locked eyes instantly and a warm smile spread across both of their faces. The bank teller, Donna, rolled her eyes when she saw Cookie walk in. She thought it was terrible the way those two flirted with each other. He was a married man, after all.

"Can I help you?" she asked with an attitude. Before Cookie could respond, Eugene stepped up.

"Don't worry about it Donna. I'll take care of her," he said.

"I'm sure you will," Donna whispered, under her breath. Cookie heard her, but chose to ignore her. As she and Eugene walked back to his office, Cookie checked him out. He was wearing a navy blue Brooks Brothers suit with a light yellow shirt and navy blue tie.

He also had on the smoothest pair of light yellow Stacy Adams shoes. As she followed him, she could smell his cologne. It happened to be one of her favorites. It was driving her crazy.

Once inside his office, Cookie sat down and crossed her legs, showing off how silky smooth they were.

"So, what can I do for you today, Miss Taylor?" he asked.

"Oh, you remembered my name? I feel so special!" she replied, blushing a little.

"Well, you are special. It was easy to remember because I haven't been able to stop thinking about you since you were here last," he admitted.

"Thank you. I can't lie, I caught myself thinking about you a couple of times this week too," Cookie said, shyly.

"I'm glad to hear that. Now, I'm going to be completely honest with you. I am married with two kids, but..."

"Yeah, I kind of figured that part out already," she said, cutting him off, pointing to the pictures on his desk.

"No doubt. As I was saying, I'm married, but since I've met you I can't stop thinking about you. I know I'm going out on a limb here, but would you like to go out for drinks sometime?" he asked.

For a few seconds Cookie was speechless. She wanted him in the worst way, but she knew that dealing with him might cause problems with Sam. But since just looking at Eugene made her panties wet, she decided to take that chance.

"Sure, we can go out for drinks, but since you are being honest, let me do the same. I have a crazy ex-boyfriend who can't accept the fact that it is over between us," she confessed.

"I'm not worried about your ex if you aren't worried about me being married," he said.

"OKAY, so when do you want to go out, Mr. Robinson?" Cookie asked, smiling.

"Are you free this weekend?" he asked.

"Yeah, I'm free all day tomorrow," she answered.

"Great. I have the perfect spot," he said, confidently.

"Where?" she asked.

"It's a surprise. Do you like surprises?" he asked.

"Of course I do. Especially big ones," she replied with a seductive smile.

"Good, then you'll love mine," he said.

"Your what?" she asked.

"My surprise. What did you think I was talking about?" he asked, laughing.

"Well, what time are you picking me up, Mr. Robinson?" she asked.

"Around 8, if that's cool with you. And please, call me Eugene,"

"And I'm Cookie. I think 8 will be fine."

"Cool, I'll be looking forward to it. If you don't mind my asking, how did you get the name, Cookie?" he asked.

"If you're a good boy, you'll find out," she said as she licked her lips.

"I'll be looking forward to that too," he replied with a smile.

Cookie gave Eugene her number and address. They made small talk as he walked her to her car.

"What should I wear tomorrow?" she asked.

"Nothing," he joked and grinned at her. "I'm just playing, but you should wear something comfortable. I'm sure you could wear a shower curtain and make it look good."

"Thanks. I think I might go get a new outfit. Oh, that reminds me, we never did get around to my check."

"I'm sorry. We started talking and I forgot I was still at work. We can go back inside really quick if you want," he said.

"No, that's alright. I'll take care of it first thing in the morning. What are the bank hours on Saturdays?" she asked.

"8am to noon," he said.

"Will you be working?"

"No, I have off Saturdays and Wednesdays. The assistant manager will be here."

"Alright. I'll see you tomorrow night. Call me if you can't make it or if you get lost," she said.

"Don't worry, I'll be there and the last thing I'll do is get lost," he said, kissing her on the cheek.

Cookie got into her car and pulled off, feeling like a teenage girl who just got asked to the prom. She decided to stop by the nail salon to get a touch up on her manicure. Once again, it was packed but she was bumped to the head of the line, as usual. Cookie wanted to get her hair done, but since she had forgotten to do anything with her check, she didn't have enough cash. She decided to call Carol to see if she had time to do anything with her hair.

"Hey Carol," she said when Carol answered her cell.

"What's up, Cookie? What are you doing?" Carol asked.

"Just leaving the salon. I'm calling to see if you can do something with my hair?" she asked.

"Girl, you know I can't do hair. I can only do braids," she said.

"That's what I wanted. Give me the Alicia Keys look," she said.

"Cookie, you got problems, but I got you," she replied, laughing.

"Thanks. I'm going home now. Just bring the clothes you're wearing tonight to my house and get dressed there," Cookie said.

"Okay," Carol said.

"Are we going to the Hot Spot, or have you changed your mind?" Cookie asked.

"No, I don't want to go there again because I don't want to run into the guy I met there last week," Carol said.

"Girl, ain't nobody tell you to leave with One Leg Larry!" Cookie said and then they both started laughing.

"I didn't know he only had one leg until we got to his place. He got undressed and took off his fake leg. Girl, it freaked me out. As soon as he hopped his one-legged ass to the bathroom, I got my stuff and left. I'm so glad I didn't give him my number. So, we gotta choose another place. I don't want to see him again," she said, laughing. Cookie was laughing so hard she almost got into a car accident.

"Cookie, it wasn't that funny!" Carol said, still laughing as well.

"I'm sorry. Don't worry, I know this poetry lounge we can go to. The people are nice and the drinks are cheap."

"Poetry lounge? Girl, I want to get my groove on not my snooze on! Look, we can decide where to go while I'm braiding your hair I'll be there in about an hour and a half," Carol said.

"Cool. I might be in the shower or taking a power nap, so just use your key and let yourself in," Cookie responded.

They hung up with each other just as Cookie was pulling into her driveway. She reached for her door handle but someone opened it before she could. Her heart dropped to her stomach as she looked up and saw Sam. She slowly got out of the car and stood face to face with him. He had a smile on his face and a box in his hand.

"Hey baby. How was your day?" he asked, as if they were a couple.

"What are you doing here, Sam?" Cookie asked, unable to keep the venom from her voice.

"Why answer a question with a question?" he joked. "Why are you here?" she asked again.

"I'm trying to be nice to you, Cookie, but you're pissing me off. I brought you a present and everything," he said. Cookie jumped when the box moved on its own. Knowing Sam, there was no telling what was inside. He tried to hand it to her, but she backed away.

"What are you afraid of? Look, I got him for you," he said, taking the lid off the box. A broad smile crossed Cookie's face as she reached in and took out a small puppy.

"Aww, it's so cute!" she said, cuddling the puppy.

"I'm glad you like him. It's a boy and his name is Sam," he said proudly.

"Why did you name him Sam?' she asked.

"So you would think of me whenever you called his name. Is that alright with you?"

"No, if he's really mine, then I want to name him," she said.

"But I wanted him to remind you of me," Sam said.

"Well, how about I name him Max?" she asked.

"Max?"

"Yeah, it's Sam backwards," she said.

"No, it's not. Sam backwards is Mas, not Max."

"It's close enough, besides, he looks like a Max."

"Okay, Mad Max and Psycho Sam," he said, laughing.

Cookie gave him a strange look and chuckled lightly.

"What kind of dog is he?" she asked. "He's a Shih-Tzu.

"A shit-what?" she asked.

"A Shih-Tzu, and he won't get much bigger than he is now. Do you like him?"

"Yes, I do. Actually, I love him. He's gonna be my little guard dog," she said happily.

"Well, he's not much of a guard dog, but he will keep you company until I move in with you." Cookie looked up sharply.

"Slow your roll, playa. I appreciate all the presents you've given me, but that doesn't mean we're getting back together. What we had before is over, Sam. I'm sorry, but it is what it is," she said forcefully.

Sam burst out laughing as if she had told the funniest joke he had ever heard. Cookie looked at him as if he had lost his mind. She turned around and walked towards her door. He jogged behind her and grabbed her by the arm.

 "What's the matter with you?" he demanded.

"I don't see what's so funny. I'm dead serious, Sam."

"I know you are. That's what's so funny. We're getting back together and you don't even know it," he said with confidence.

"Whatever," Cookie replied as she used the key to unlock her door and go in. Sam walked in behind her. She shot him a crazy look.

"What do you think you're doing, Sam? I didn't invite you in."

"You didn't say it, but you were thinking it," he replied smugly.

"Not really. Besides, I have company on the way over."

"Who you got coming over? That old ass white guy?" he asked.

"It's none of your business who I invite to my house. And it was really messed up what you did to his car," she added.

"I don't know what you are talking about," Sam said with a plastic smile.

"Don't play stupid with me. You know exactly what I'm talking about."

"I really don't. That's my story and I'm sticking to it. But, since you got lover boy coming over, I think I might stick around for a little while," he said, sitting down on her couch. Cookie was about to protest, but the puppy started barking. She took him out of the box and let him run around the living room. He went right over to the entertainment center, squatted and started to go to the bathroom on the rug.

"Max!! What are you doing? No! Bad dog!" Cookie yelled. Sam laughed as she got something to clean up the mess. "This ain't gonna work, Max, if you're gonna pee and poop all over the place!" she said.

"What do you expect from a puppy? You have to train him."

"They didn't have already trained puppies where you got him?" she asked.

"Nah, but I'll help you train him," he said, laughing.

"That's alright, I'll work it out. On another note, I really think you should be leaving. I have to take a shower and get ready for tonight."

"What do you see in that old guy?" he asked.

"For your information, he's my co-worker and we're just friends. Besides, I'm not even going out with him tonight, Carol and I are having a girl's night out," she answered honestly.

"Yeah, whatever. You don't gotta lie to me," he said.

"What do I have to lie to you for? We are no longer together, I don't have to explain myself to you," Cookie said, with attitude.

"I'm sorry, baby, I didn't come over to upset you. I just get a little crazy when it comes to you. I can't help it."

Cookie felt herself softening up. Sam could be so sweet and sincere at times.

She changed the subject before she could fall into his trap.

"What do puppies eat? Did you bring any food for Max?" she asked.

"Yeah, I brought a few different brands of puppy food for him. You can test them out to see what he likes best," he answered.

"Sam, do you have a job? Because I don't see how you can afford all these gifts that you keep bringing me, if you just came home from jail," she pointed out.

"You know I ain't the working type, but I got my ways of getting money. And, no, I don't sell drugs and none of it is stolen," he replied. Cookie smiled and shook her head.

She picked up Max and sat down on the couch next to Sam.

"So, where are you staying?" she asked.

"With my sister," he replied.

"Oh, how is she doing?"

"She's alright, but she still doesn't like you," he pointed out, smiling.

"I'm sure, and the feeling's mutual," she said with a smile of her own.

Their small talk was interrupted by the opening of the front door. Carol walked in with a small bag in one hand and her clothes in the other.

"Cookie, why did you leave your door unlocked? Girl, you know there are all kinds of--," her sentenced stopped short for a second at the sight of Sam. "All kinds of crazy people around here," she continued, looking directly at Sam.

"Hey Carol. That was a fast hour and a half," Cookie said, getting up from the couch.

"Actually, I'm only 15 minutes early," Carol said.

"Oh, sure," responded Cookie.

"Yeah...What is he doing here?" Carol asked, pointing at Sam. He wanted to tell Carol to mind her own business, but he was trying to stay on Cookie's good side, so he let it go.

"Sam got me a puppy. Look, isn't he cute?" Cookie said, lifting Max up for Carol to see.

"Yeah, he's alright," Carol said, without even looking at the dog. She added, "Cookie, can I talk to you for a second?"

Carol and Cookie walked into the kitchen to talk. Sam got off of the couch and slowly crept towards the kitchen to eaves drop.

"Girl, I don't know what's going on, but I don't think it's a good idea to have him around. You know how insane he is," Carol said.

"You're right, but like I said, he just came by to give me Max."

"Who the hell is Max?" asked Carol.

"This is Max," she said, holding up the small puppy.

"So, now he's trying to buy his way back into your life? Wake up and smell the coffee girl, before it's too late," she said, trying to convince her friend of her mistake.

"Don't worry. I have everything under control. I already told him that I don't have any plans on getting back together with him," Cookie replied.

"Cookie, please. Do you really think that he'll take no for an answer? Cut all ties while you still can!" pleaded Carol.

Sam was furious and wanted to run into the kitchen and choke the life out of Carol, but he kept his cool. He calmly walked into the kitchen.

"I don't mean to interrupt, but I have to get going. You have a good time tonight, Cookie, and I'll catch up to you later," he didn't give her time to respond.

He turned around and left. Both Cookie and Carol were shocked and speechless. Carol was surprised that he left without being forced and Cookie was wondering how much of their conversation he had heard.

*   *   *

After doing their hair, showering and getting dressed, they finally decided on going back to the Hot Spot, even though Carol was risking running into One Leg Larry. She would just have to take that chance. It was either that or go to the poetry lounge. Both girls were dressed to kill.

Carol had on an all-black cat suit that hugged each curve just right along with tall boots that reached her knees to compliment the look. Cookie chose to dress comfortably. She had on a tight pair of Baby Phat jeans. So tight, in fact, that she had needed to lie down on her bed just to get them on. She wore a pink Baby Phat top with a matching jean jacket with rhinestones. To finish her outfit just right, she wore Timberland stilettos.

Once again, they knew they would be the hottest chicks in the club.

CHAPTER 4

The next morning, Cookie woke up with a terrible headache. She had one too many cranberry and vodka's the night before. She looked at her alarm clock and saw that it was already 11 o'clock. She only had an hour to get ready and make it to the bank before they closed. Cookie tried to get up but just couldn't make herself. She laid back down and fell asleep.

By the time she woke up again, it was five pm. Max was curled up next to her, licking himself. She was a little upset because she wouldn't have any cash for the weekend, unless she used her ATM card and dipped into her savings, which she didn't like to do unless she had to.

She was also annoyed because she only had three hours until her date with Eugene and she wanted to go out and buy a new outfit. Cookie stumbled to the bathroom. On her way there she noticed traces of Max marking his new territory.

There were little puddles of pee and clumps of poop everywhere. She just shook her head as she made her way to the shower.

*   *   *

After a 40 minute shower, she threw on some clothes, cleaned up after Max and straightened up her house. She finally fed Max and he tore through it so fast that she decided to give him another bowl.

 "Sorry, Max. I forgot to feed you. I promise Mommy won't let it happen again," she said, patting him on the head. Once he finished eating, she took him out for a short walk. As she stepped outside, she thought she saw Sam driving by but she wasn't sure. Cookie laughed at Max as he chased a butterfly.

*   *   *

Around eight pm, Eugene knocked on Cookie's door. When she opened the door in her peach Chanel dress, he took a step back and smiled like a man who had just won the lottery. Cookie spun around so he could get a full view.

"Do you like?" she asked, still modeling for him.

"Meee liike," he replied, trying – and failing – to sound like a caveman.

She chuckled lightly at his silliness. Eugene pulled a dozen peach colored roses from behind his back and handed them to her.

"Oh, they're so beautiful! And they match my dress! How did you know I would be wearing this color?" she asked, amazed.

"Great minds think alike," he said.

"Yes, they do," she said, blushing.

"So, Miss Taylor, are you ready for a fun-filled evening?"

"Yes, I am, but first, let me put these gorgeous flowers in some water. And I thought I asked you to call me Cookie."

"You did. I almost forgot that I'm supposed to be a good boy so I can get a bite of that Cookie," he said, mischievously.

"That's right," she said, smiling. "Come in while I get my purse and put these flowers in some water."

On the way to Eugene's mystery place, Cookie was anxious since she had no idea where he was taking her. She asked for hints, but he just turned on the radio and told her to listen. Jill Scott's first cd was playing. She listened for a while, but didn't catch any clues, so she made small talk with him as he drove. They got to know each other a little better during the 30 minute drive.

They pulled into the parking lot of a shopping center. Cookie knew where she was and was hoping they were going to the place she had in mind.

"Surprise! We're here!" Eugene said, excited.

"Where is here?"

"Right over there. The Poetry Lounge. I know you like to party, so I hope you don't mind a little change of pace. My cousin Eric owns the place and tonight Jill Scott is performing." Cookie beamed with joy. She couldn't contain her excitement.

"Have you been reading my diary or something, because I've been trying to get my girl Carol to come here with me?"

"Once again, great minds think alike," Eugene said, smoothly.

Eugene had reserved a table for the two of them, right next to the stage. The place was dimly lit and had a nice, relaxed vibe to it. They ordered a shrimp appetizer and two cocktails. Eric let him know that everything was on the house, but Cookie didn't want to drink too much after the hangover she had woken up with that morning.

The poets were smooth and laid back and Cookie was having a really nice time. She was shocked when the M.C. called Eugene's name to perform next. He stood up, smoothed out his slacks and kissed Cookie on the cheek. She smiled as he went up and grabbed the mic.

"Good evening, ladies and gentlemen. This poem is called 'Good Cookies'. It's dedicated to the beautiful lady in the front row in the peach dress. I just wrote it last night, so bear with me," Eugene said calmly.

I'm in love with Good Cookies,
 but not the Oreo kind.
So I examine your body,
 while exploring your mind.

In search of what more I can find,
 but you're perfect.
Patience is a virtue,
 so my waiting is worth it.
I know you can work it,
I can tell by your walk.
I look into your eyes,
 and I'm compelled by your thoughts.
When you're done with that chair,
 can you please sit on my face next?
I love your Good Cookies,
 and I ain't even had a taste yet.

After listening to the poem, Cookie had tears in her eyes. Everyone was on their feet, clapping and whistling. When he jumped off the stage and returned to her side, she gave him a warm hug and a soft kiss on his lips. A few minutes later Jill Scott stepped on stage and the crowd went crazy.

  "Thank you, thank you. But give it up one more time to the gentlemen and his poem! He had me getting hot back stage! I had to fan myself just to cool off!" she said to her audience. The crowd gave him another round of applause. Jill Scott started off with some spoken word poetry of her own before she began to perform. She did a mix of her old and newest songs, which the audience loved. After the concert, Cookie and Eugene were able to go back stage to meet her, where they sat for a while and chatted. Eugene thanked his cousin Eric and they left.

*　　　*　　　*

On the way back home, Cookie was silent and in deep thought. She seemed to have a lot in common with Eugene and she was feeling him already, but Cookie knew he was a married man. So, a relationship between the two of them could only go so far. But she was having a great time, and didn't want the night to end just yet.

Eugene was thinking about Cookie as well, and didn't want the date to end yet either.

"Penny for your thoughts?" he asked.

"I was just thinking what a wonderful time I've had tonight. I almost don't want it to end," she replied.

"Well, it doesn't have to. Are you hungry?"

"Yeah, a little bit," Cookie replied.

"I know this spot not too far from here called 'Quita's Place'. The food is great," he said.

"Sounds good to me."

Over a plate of steak and potatoes, they shared a great conversation. They found out that they had a lot in common. They really enjoyed each other's company.

After dinner they shared a slice of pecan pie with ice cream. Cookie spoon fed him a few bites and he returned the favor.

They left the restaurant and headed back to Cookie's house. Once they got there, they both sat in the car silently for a few seconds. Neither of them wanted the other one to leave.

"I had a really good time tonight Eugene," Cookie said, breaking the awkward silence.

"Yeah, me too, Cookie. Maybe we can get together again sometime soon."

"Sure, I'd like that a lot." Cookie gave him a kiss on the cheek. She got out of the car and waved goodbye. Eugene stared at her plump backside as she walked away. She fiddled with her keys at the door. She wanted to invite him in, but she didn't want to come off as too fast, so she just blew him a kiss and went inside. Eugene smiled to himself and drove off.

*　　*　　*

On the way to his house, he tried to think of a story he could tell his wife. He told her he was going to a bar to watch the game with a few of his college buddies, but it was almost two o'clock in the morning. The game had been over hours ago and the bar was closed.

I don't know what I'm going to tell Linda. I just hope she's asleep when I get there, he thought.

As he pulled into his driveway he saw that all the lights in the house were off. He slowly got out of his car and went inside as quietly as he could. He checked on his kids and saw that they were both sound asleep. Eugene was still a little wired so he took a quick shower. Afterwards, he looked in the mirror and thought about Cookie and how great the night had been. He knew he was playing with fire by going out with her, but there was something about Cookie that was making him risk losing his marriage and his family. He slipped in between the covers of his bed, trying not to wake his wife.

"How was the game, baby?" she asked, snuggling closer to him. Eugene was caught off guard and he mentally cursed himself for waking her.

"It...It was okay," he stuttered. Linda sensed something was wrong so she sat up and looked at the alarm clock.

"It's 2:30 am. How long have you been here?" she asked, turning on the light.

"For a while, why?"

"How long is a while?"

"Long enough to check on the kids and take a shower."

"What did you do after the game?"

"Me and the fella's just kicked it at the bar for a little bit and then we went to the strip club," he lied.

"What?! You went to a strip club? I can't believe you!" Linda screamed.

"Listen, baby, after the game, Mike wanted to treat Darren to a Pre-bachelor's party, so we hit the strip club. Don't be mad at me. I'm being honest and open with you. Gimme a little bit of credit," Eugene said, planting wet kisses on Linda's neck.

"Don't...do....that," Linda said, breathing heavily.

"I'm glad you're awake, because after a few drinks and seeing naked girls I couldn't wait to come home and make love to you."

"But... Gene.... I... I..."

"Don't say nothing, baby, just relax," he said, taking off her nightgown and kissing her stomach. Linda grabbed his head as he traveled down between her legs where he kissed her through her panties. She moaned and ground herself into his face. He quickly pulled her panties off and slipped two fingers inside her. He moved his fingers in and out while sucking on her clit. She continued to rotate her hips and fondle her breast.

"Oh... Oh... Gene... Don't stop... Please.... Don't stop." she yelled. Eugene was turned on by her excitement. He pushed her legs up and she held them in the air by grabbing her ankles. He repositioned himself, and dove in face first. He worked his tongue like he was trying to win a prize. Linda screamed in pleasure as she came and her whole body began to shake. She rested her legs on his shoulders.

"Damn baby, you're gonna have to go to the strip club more often, if you're gonna come home and do me like this." Linda said smiling as she gestured for Eugene to come to her. He gladly obeyed, crawling on the bed while planting soft kisses on the way up, Linda kissed him passionately as she guided his shaft inside of her.

She gasped as he entered with slow long strokes. Linda arched her back, giving him the ability to go deeper. Eugene was on the verge of an early exit so he stopped and switched positions. He stood up and pulled his wife to the edge of the bed. With her legs spread and her ankles in each one of his hands, he slipped inside her again. She gripped the bed sheets tighter with each thrust. He sped up and slowed down repeatedly. Linda was on the verge of another orgasm. She begged for him not to stop, and he didn't plan to. He pumped faster and she screamed louder. She came again but with more force then the first two. Eugene finally reached his climax and collapsed on top of her.

"Damn Cookie that was the best." Eugene panted, out of breath.

"What did you call me?"

"Nothing." He said nervously.

"It sounded like you called me cookie. Where did that come from?"

"I meant to say that was the best cookie. I know you don't like for me to curse. I was just saying that it was great, that's all."

"Calm down baby. You don't have to get all defensive. I like being called your cookie. You haven't used a pet name for me in a long time. I thought it was sweet." She said kissing him softly.

Eugene laid down while Linda went to get a hot cloth.

What am I going to do? That was a close call and next time I might not be so lucky. I gotta do something about the Cookie situation. She got me tripping and I ain't even hit it yet, he thought to himself.

CHAPTER 5

ookie woke up Sunday afternoon with Max snuggled up next to her. She stretched and a huge smile spread across her face as she thought about her date with Eugene. He was tall, dark, and handsome. Charming with a good head on his shoulders, and an even better job. The only down side was him being married. Her thoughts were interrupted by the sound of the phone ringing. She got out the bed and answered without checking the caller id.

"Hello," she said cheerfully.

"Hello to you too Miss Cookie. Don't we sound chipper today?" The smile on her face disappeared.

"Oh... Hey Tony." She said flatly.

"Wow, your mood changed quickly. I guess you were expecting someone else." He replied.

"What's going on Tony? I was about to get in the shower."

"That sounds fun. Can I join you?"

"I don't know. Ask your wife if it's ok." She shot back.

"Ouch, that hurt. But you remember what happened the last time we took a shower together."

Cookie didn't respond, she just smiled to herself.

"Anyway, I just called to see if we were still on for the night." Tony said casually.

"Yeah. I almost forgot."

"Wow, you forgot about me. Now I'm really hurt."

"You know it ain't like that. I just have a lot on my mind right now." Cookie said.

"I understand." He replied dryly. "Well, what do you have in mind? You know it's a school night and I can't stay out too late."

"It's ok. I promise to have you back before your curfew."

"Alright, what do you want to do?"

"You." Tony quickly replied.

"Come on now I told you that--"
"I know, I know, it was just a joke. I thought maybe we could go see that new Tom Cruise movie. And afterwards we could have dinner at Chateau Blu'."

"Chateau Blu'. Is that the new French restaurant downtown?"

"It sure is. So what do you say?"

"I say, I'll be ready by 7 o'clock." Cookie told him.

"Great I'll see you then." Tony said happily, before he hung up the phone.

He turned around and his wife was standing in the doorway.

"Hey honey," he said with a nervous smile.

"Don't 'hey honey' me. Who were you just talking to?" She asked with an attitude.

*   *   *

Cookie was lounging on the couch with Max. She had on sweat pants and an oversized t-shirt. She was watching Law & Order when the doorbell rang, but she waited until the commercial, before she got up to answer the door.

"What Tony?"

"I'm so, so sorry baby. I know you're pissed about me being late but--"

"Late. Tony it's almost ten o'clock and you were supposed to be here at seven. So late is an understatement."

"You're right, but let me explain." He pleaded.

"I don't want to hear it. I already ate, so going out to eat is not an option. I'm too tired to go watch a movie, plus I have to get up early for work, so let's try this another time."

"Cookie you don't understand what I had to go through to--"

"And it doesn't matter." She said cutting him off.

"But my wife--"

"Tony, its ok. We can go out some other time. It's not that big of a deal."

"Alright, well can I at least come in for a while?"

"Not tonight. I told you I'm tired, and as soon as my show finishes, I'm going to sleep." Cookie yawned.

"Going to sleep with whom? I know you got somebody else in there. That's why you're blowing me off."

"Whatever you say, Tony. You're the one that showed up three hours late and you're accusing me of blowing you off. Puh-lease. I don't have time for this. I'm missing Law & Order, so I'll see you at work tomorrow." Cookie said with an attitude.

Tony looked like all the air had been taken out of his balloon. It had been over a week since he'd last been with Cookie and he was fiending.

"Come on baby. Just let me chill for a little bit." Cookie didn't respond, she frowned and shook her head.

"It's not that late, we can still do something," he pleaded with her.

"You just don't quit do you?" She smirked.

"You know how we do baby. Cookies and Milk."

"Well, not tonight Mr. Milk."

"How bout we--"

"How bout we see each other tomorrow."

"Ok. Can I at least use the bathroom?"

Cookie let him in to use the bathroom. She knew he just wanted to see if she was alone or not, but she didn't care.
When he came out the bathroom, she was sitting on the couch. He sat down and she stood up and walked towards the door.

"No need to get comfortable. I told you I'm going to sleep. And now that you've seen that there is no one else here, you can go." She politely told him. Tony smiled and gave her a kiss on the cheek before leaving. Cookie closed and locked the door, lay back on the couch and finished watching TV, until she fell asleep. Around 1am, her phone started ringing. She jumped up and answered it.

"Hello?" She said, groggily.

"I'm sorry. Did I wake you?" The caller asked. At the sound of his voice, Cookie perked up and a smile spread across her face.

"Yeah I was sleep, but I'm up now. What's going on?"

"I was just calling to let you know I had a real good time yesterday, and I hope we can go out again sometime soon." Eugene said.

"I had a wonderful time also and yes I would love to hang out with you again."

"Cool. Now that I've heard that sweet voice of yours, I can get some sleep." Cookie smiled so hard that her cheeks started hurting. "Well I never did deposit my check so if you'll be at work I will see you tomorrow. Maybe we can go to a bar for happy hour."

"That would be great. I will see you tomorrow Miss Taylor. I mean Cookie." They hung up from each other and she couldn't go back to sleep, so she got up to take a hot bath.

*   *   *

While laid back in the tub, she lit a few candles and had the soft sounds of Floetry playing through the speakers. Her mind drifted to Eugene and her hands traveled towards her sex. She used two fingers and slowly rubbed her clit. She let out a soft moan while her free hand massaged her hard nipples. Cookie was on the brink of an orgasm as she screamed Eugene's name. After a few minutes she caught her breath and finished washing. About 20 minutes later, she and Max were cuddled up in the bed.

*   *   *

The following day Cookie was at work. Little Tommy Mitchell was acting up and wouldn't listen.

"You're not my mom. I don't have to take orders from you."

"Tommy if you don't fix your attitude. I'm sending you to the principal's office." She said.

"I don't care, y'all can both kiss my ass." He shouted defiantly.

"That's it, Mr. Mitchell, Go to the principal's office." She yelled.

After school let out, Cookie called Tommy's parents.

"Hello may I speak to the parents of Tommy Mitchell."

"Yes, speaking. How may I help you?"

"My name is Miss Taylor, I'm Tommy's math teacher. I'm calling because he was very disruptive in class today. First, he started out by bullying the other students. Then in his exact words, he told me to 'kiss his ass'. He was sent to see the principal but I don't know what actions were taken."

"Well, thank you, Miss Taylor. When his father comes home, we will take care of it. And I'm sorry for my son's behavior."

"Don't worry about it. Tommy is a bright student. I know he can do better if he applies himself." Cookie said reassuringly.

"Thank you again for calling."

"No Problem."

Cookie hung up the phone feeling a little better but still not quite convinced that the call did any good. She packed up her things and went to go deposit her check. A smile spread across her face as she thought about seeing Eugene again.

*   *   *

She pulled into the lot and parked next to his money green B.M.W 7.50. Cookie checked out herself in the mirror, nodded in approval and went inside. As soon as she walked in, Donna and her locked eyes. Donna had a customer so Cookie went to the next teller. She was an older lady who looked to be in her early 60's.

"How may I assist you today?" She asked with a warm smile.

"I would like to deposit this check."

"Sure, all I need is your ID and account number."

Cookie searched her purse before realizing that she left her wallet in the desk at work.

"I'm sorry I don't have my ID, but Mr. Robinson knows me."

"I'm sure he does." Donna interjected from the next booth, with an attitude. As if on cue, Eugene came from the back.

"Hello, Miss Taylor. Pleasant surprise." He said winking his eye.

"Hey Mr. Robinson. I came to deposit my check, but I forgot my ID again." Cookie replied.

"That's not a problem. Follow me to my office." As soon as the doors closed, Cookie grabbed Eugene by his tie and pulled him in for a wet kiss.

"Wow, what was that for?" He asked with a smile.

"Because I've been thinking about you all day, and I couldn't wait to kiss you."

"Well, I can't wait to taste you." Eugene replied.

"What did you say?"

"Oh... I said... I said I can't even hate you."

"Whatever. I heard you the first time freak nasty." Cookie said jokingly.

After depositing her check, Cookie and Eugene made plans to hook up in a few hours

*   *   *

Tony stayed after school a little later than usual. He finally packed up and left around 6:30pm. He walked outside and noticed there were only a few cars in the parking lot. He unlocked the door and threw his brief case in the back seat. When he turned around, he was staring down the barrel of a .38 special.

"I don't have a lot of cash on me, but I do have credit cards and you can have them all. Just don't kill me." Tony pleaded, dangling the car keys in front of him.

"I don't want your money or your car!" Sam yelled, smacking the keys out of Tony's hand.

"Then, what the hell do you want?"

Sam hit Tony on the side of his head with the butt of the gun. He fell to one knee and grabbed his head as blood trickled down his face.

"I ask the questions. You answer by nodding or shaking your head. Do we have an understanding?" Tony nodded yes.

"Do you know Natasha Taylor?" Tony didn't answer, he just gave Sam a blank stare, so he hit him again.

"I said, do you know Cookie?"

"Yes I know her. We work tog--" was all Tony could get out before he got smacked in the face.

"I said, don't talk. Just nod or shake your head. Now don't lie to me. Are you sleeping with her?" Tony thought about his answer before finally shaking his head no. Sam got frustrated and drew his fist back to hit him again, but Tony flinched and braced himself for the blow. Sam laughed and continued to question him.

"I already know what's going on between you two. I thought you were smart enough to take the hint last time you were at her house, but noooooo. You were there again last night. Lucky you didn't stay there long or I would have messed this car up too." Sam said, kicking the driver side door.

"Y...Y...You're Psycho Sam. I swear Cookie and I are just friends nothing more. We jus--" Sam cut him off mid-sentence by sticking the barrel of the gun in his mouth.

"I told you not to talk. Now suck on this and listen. If I catch you wit my girl again, I will kill you. As a matter of fact, I'm going to let you live, but I will put a hurting on your pretty wife, Sarah. Oh yeah, I know where you live – 57 Hawthorne street. Don't look so surprised. I do my homework. Stay away from Cookie, if you see her in the hallways, don't say anything to her. Don't even look her way. Are we clear on that?" Tony nodded his head slightly with the gun still in his mouth, afraid it would go off.

"Good, now go home and make love to your wife and keep away from my girl, or I promise that my face will be the last face that Sarah ever sees. I know you wouldn't want that to happen. I watched y'all two Saturday night while y'all were having sex in the pool. Man, she's a screamer." Sam said laughing. He pushed Tony to the ground and then jogged away.

Tony stood up and brushed himself off. He looked around in amazement as he watch Sam jump in a pickup truck and speed off. Tony started to call the police, but quickly changed his mind when he thought about Sam knowing his address.

Damn messing with her, I put my family in jeopardy as well as my marriage. On top of that I almost got killed. I really gotta keep my hand out that cookie jar.

CHAPTER 6

"**H**ey baby, I'm hanging out with the fellas tonight. I had a long day and we are getting a few drinks." Eugene told his wife.

"Again Eugene? Y'all just went out a couple nights ago."

"I know but like I said I had a rough day. Besides you weren't complaining, when I came home from the strip club and we went at it like two teenagers."

A smile crept onto Linda's face as she thought about their passionate night of lustful sex.

"You're right. I am still a little sore. Anyway, how long are you gonna be? I made your favorite for dinner."

"We are going to happy hour at Maddies, so I should be home by 8 o'clock, no later than 9. Keep my plate warm for me, and soak that sore kitty in the tub, because after dinner I want dessert." Eugene said seductively.

"Whatever you say daddy... Just don't keep me waiting too long." Linda purred.

Eugene hung up the phone feeling a little relieved that he had bought himself some time. He calmly walked out of the bathroom and sat next to Cookie at the bar.

"Is everything ok on the home front?" She asked.

"Yeah, everything's cool. I told her I'd be home by 9pm, so it's all good."

"Well... We got about 3 hours until then, so let's finish these drinks and get out of here." Cookie said.

"You're so cool, it's amazing. I love it that you're so understanding and easy to talk to. I feel so free around you. You're like a breath of fresh air." Eugene said looking in her eyes. Cookie was lost for words, so she held up her glass.

"Let's toast... To us... And being on the same page." She said, clinking glasses and a wink of the eye. They left the bar and headed to Cookie's house.

*   *   *

She put on the soft sounds of Marvin Gaye, while Eugene sat nervously on the couch. After a few minutes, she sashayed downstairs wearing pink Victoria's Secret lingerie. Eugene's eyes popped as she stood in front of him and danced seductively to Marvin Gaye's 'Let's get it on'. She then straddled his lap and whispered in his ear,

"I got a batch of fresh baked Cookies, made just for you."

"Mmm... I love cookies" he whispered back. Cookie kissed him with so much passion, that it made his heart skip a beat. Not even his wife had ever kissed him like that. He kissed her back with just as much intensity.

She slowly took off his shirt and kissed his chest. Her soft lips caused him to let out a light moan. Cookie smiled to herself as she slid off his lap and on to her knees. She unbuckled his belt and pulled off his pants.

"My, aren't we a big boy," she said, looking at his shaft as it poked through the opening in his boxers. He smiled proudly and slid his underwear off. Cookie licked her lips and took him into her mouth. It seemed like his already hard manhood grew even more as she worked it.

"Baby, what are you trying to do to me?" He moaned in pleasure. Cookie grabbed the head of his shaft and licked it slowly before taking him in as far as she could. Eugene's body got stiff and Cookie knew he was on the verge of an orgasm. So she stopped and stood up. He was still sitting on the couch trying to catch his breath when he pulled Cookie in between his legs. He kissed her stomach, causing her knees to buckle. She slowly eased out of her panties and pushed her sex into his face. He happily accepted as his warm tongue slid across her clit. He grabbed her waist and picked her up just high enough so she could put her left leg over his right shoulder. Then she put her right leg over his left shoulder. He placed his hands on her lower back to hold her steady and keep her from falling backwards.

Her sex smelled like vanilla, but it tasted like chocolate and honey. She tasted so good that he licked her creamy center until his mouth hurt. He laid her on the carpet and continued to pleasure her orally. Cookie couldn't take it anymore and she was begging for him to be inside of her.

After a few more minutes, he granted her wish and slowly guided his shaft inside of her. Cookie was so tight and wet that he felt like he was going to cum as soon as he entered her. He worked his manhood little by little until the whole ten inches fit snuggly inside. She gently bit his shoulder as he went deeper. Eugene took his time, enjoying every stroke. Cookie quietly moaned in his ear, getting him even more excited. After a while, she got on her knees and rested her elbows on the couch. He penetrated her from behind, causing her to grip the sofa cushions. She screamed his name, as he grunted hers.

*　　*　　*

Sam was outside looking through Cookie's window while some guy was sexing her from the back. He was furious as he paced back and forth. He stopped and looked inside her house again, and Cookie was throwing it back and biting her bottom lip. Sam couldn't watch anymore. He went to his truck and grabbed a crow bar from behind the seat. He walked over to the green B.M.W and used the crow bar to loosen the lug nuts on all four tires. Then he went back to the window and saw the guy sitting on the couch with Cookie riding him backwards.

She had her head down, but when she looked up, she locked eyes with Sam... She jumped as he threw the crow bar through the window, scaring her and causing her to fall back into Eugene. By the time, they got up and ran to the door, all they saw were the tail lights of Sam's pickup truck as he sped down the street.

*   *   *

"Who the hell was that?" Eugene asked. Cookie didn't answer him, she just ran upstairs to put some clothes on. When she came back down stairs, he was dressed as well.

"I'm so sorry Eugene. That was the crazy ex-boyfriend I was telling you about."

"Why would he throw a crowbar through your window?"

"He was watching us having sex, and when I noticed him, that's when he broke the window. I truly apologize, but I think you should go, just in case he comes back." Cookie said sweeping up the broken glass.

"Don't worry about me. I can handle myself. I'm more concerned about you. Is there anywhere you can go for the night?"

"Yeah, I could go to my girl Carol's house, but I won't. He's crazy but he's not stupid enough to do anything to me. I'll be alright." Eugene hung around until ten thirty. He helped her clean up and they ordered take out. He also duct taped a trash bag over the window.

"You know you're going to have to replace that glass as soon as possible." Eugene told her as they walked to his car.

"Yeah I am. As a matter of fact I'm gonna take off work tomorrow and get it done. I can't leave my house with a trash bag covering the window. This is a nice neighborhood, but if the wrong person notices a broken window and nobody home, I'm sure they won't hesitate to go inside and rob me." Cookie said looking at his B.M.W, glad that Pyscho Sam didn't do any damage to it.

 "So, tell me, Miss Taylor are we going to get a chance to finish what we started or is this where we call it quits?"

 "I told you about my crazy ex. I just didn't think he would do something like this. So if you want to continue to see me, even though I kinda have this rain cloud following me it's totally up to you. Of course I would like to finish what we started, but the ball is in your court." Cookie said.

 "Well I'm not scared of the crow bar bandit." He joked. "And yes, I want to continue seeing you. There's something about Cookie that I can't enough of." Eugene pulled her close and kissed her deeply.

 "So when will I see you again Mr. Robinson?"

"How about tomorrow?" He replied with a smile.

"Wow, two days in a row. Aren't I the lucky one?"

"No, I'm the lucky one."

"If you want, you can come over on your lunch break, and we can have a picnic in my back yard," Cookie said.

"That'll be great. Do you want me to bring anything?"

"Nah I got everything covered, but if you do want to bring anything, just surprise me."

"Cool. What time should I be here?"

"What time and how long is your lunch break?"

"I'm the boss, baby. I can take my break whenever and stay out as long as I want." Eugene said with a smile.

"Ok then, Mr. Boss Man. Be here at 12:30 sharp."

"I will be here at 12:29," he said, kissing her before getting in his car.

After watching him drive away, Cookie went back inside her house and called Carol.

"Hey girl, what you doing?" Cookie asked.

"Well, me and my man was about to get our freak on."

"Oh, tell Nigel I said hi."

"Well... Mm... H... He's not allowed t-t-to talk with a mouth full, but he sends his love."

"Y'all so nasty. Girl call me back when y'all done. I gotta tell you what Sam's crazy ass did while I was getting my freak on with Eugene." Cookie said.

"What you finally got it on with Eugene?" Carol yelled, pushing Nigel's head away.

"Yeah and Sam ruined it. Call me back so I can fill you in on what happened."

"Hold on Nigel. Let me talk to my girl for a minute... Don't be mad. I promise that Mommy will take care of you. Just give me a little bit... Ok Cookie, tell me what went down and don't leave out anything. You know I need details so I can have the visual."

"Ok, Eugene and I went out for happy hour, and when we got back to my place, giiiiirl... He threw it on me. He ate my cookie so good, I was begging him to stop! He was sitting on the couch with my cat in his face and he tore it up. Then he put his long pipe inside of me and I almost fainted. His stroke is serious. I swear I felt the tip of his shaft touch my heart." Cookie said jokingly.

"Girl you are too much, but please tell me where Sam fits into this story, because all this talk about sex got me ready to call Nigel back in here and finish what we started."

"I'm sorry, but you said you wanted details, and that man can work his wood. Anyway I was riding him reverse cowgirl style, on the couch in the living room. When I looked up, can you believe that Sam was looking through the window, staring at us?"

"Are you for real?" Carol asked in amazement.

"Yes and, when he realized that I saw him, the fool had the nerve to throw a crow bar through my window. By the time I ran to the door, he drove off. I felt so embarrassed, but Eugene made me feel better. He stayed around for a while to help me clean up. Then we ate Chinese food and watched TV, until he had to get home to his wife."

"Well did y'all at least finish the sex session?" Carol asked.

"No we didn't, but I'm taking off work tomorrow and he's coming over for lunch and dessert."

"Damn, Cookie. What do you do to these guys, to have them going crazy, and leaving their wives over you?" Carol said laughing.

"I'll tell you my secret. It's my good cookies. I don't have that name for no reason."

"Girl, please, you got that name because you're half black, half white like an Oreo. And when you were growing up, the kids teased you by calling you, Oreo cookie. That's how you got the name." Carol said sarcastically.

"Whatever, but I *kept* the name because of this ill, nana I got. You think I'm playing. Every other night, I take a bath filled with white wine vinegar, chocolate powder, honey, and vanilla syrup. That's how I bake the cookies."

"What?! You are off the chain! Talking about baking the cookies. So I guess the vinegar, chocolate, honey, and vanilla are the ingredients and the hot bath water is the oven."

"Pretty much. The vanilla is for the scent, the chocolate and honey is for the taste and the vinegar is to keep it tight and clean. I don't play no games when it comes to my cookies. That's why married men can't get enough of me and single men want to marry me."

"Cookie, you are something else, But I can't even front because I'm gonna try that. I already wrote down the recipe." Carol said laughing. They talked for a few more minutes before hanging up with each other.

CHAPTER 7

Cookie had just finished preparing everything for the picnic, when the doorbell rang. She looked out the bedroom window, she couldn't see anybody, all she saw was a crème colored Chrysler 300M. She walked down stairs and looked out the peep hole. A huge smile spread across her face as she seen Eugene standing outside.

Cookie opened the door, and her sight zoomed in on the bandage over his right eye. She assumed that he and his wife got into a fight over him coming home late. *I hope he's not the type to hit women*, she thought to herself while giving him a hug.

"Aww poor baby what happen to your face?"

"It's a long story. I'll tell you about it over lunch." He said kissing her on the forehead.

"Okay" Cookie said, fearing that her assumptions may be true.

"I see you got the window fixed already."

"Yeah I wanted it to be done before you got here. I don't want any interruptions during our picnic. And by the way, you're quite early, I was just about to get in the shower."

"Sorry about that. I meant to call you and let you know that I was on my way. I went to work, but I left early and took off the rest of the day. My wife thinks I'm working, so I'm all yours for as long as you want me." Eugene said, smiling.

"Well everything is ready. I just need to jump in the shower. Make yourself comfortable. I'll be back down in about 15 minutes. But if you get lonely, the bathroom door will be unlocked," she said with a wink.

Eugene went out to his car and grabbed a giant size teddy bear. He took it in the house and set it on the couch. He then crept upstairs and slowly opened the bathroom door.

"Hey, Miss Taylor. I just came up to see if you needed any help."

"Sure, I can always use an extra pair of hands, but I'm almost done, so you can help me dry off," Cookie said seductively.

"I think I can handle that."

He waited for her to step out of the shower, and then wrapped the towel around her body. He started with her arms, then her back. Eugene bent down on one knee and dried off her legs. She smelled so good, that he couldn't resist kissing her inner thigh. Her knees felt weak as he placed soft kisses so close to her sex. Cookie sat down on the fuzzy covered toilet seat. Eugene continued to pleasure her by sliding his warm tongue across her clit.

She was moaning his name, begging him not to stop, but he did just the opposite. He replaced the clit with her toes as he kissed and sucked each one. Cookie finished the job that had Eugene started by using her own two fingers to stimulate her hot spot. The feeling of him sucking her toes, while she played with herself was driving her insane. Eugene placed her foot down and put his face back in her lap, just in time for her to release her sweet nectar in his mouth.

"Baby, you taste so good, I could eat this all day," he said, wiping his chin. "By the way you eat these cookies; you can have them whenever you get hungry." She replied jokingly.

"Well now that I've had dessert, what's up with lunch?"

"Let me get dressed real quick and I got you. I hope you like roast beef sandwiches."

"I'll like whatever you have for me." He said playfully smacking her backside. "I'll be downstairs waiting for you, unless you need help getting dressed."

"No that's Okay, but after lunch I will need your help getting undressed," she said smiling.

About ten minutes later, Cookie walked downstairs in a baby blue Rocawear sweat suit. Her hair was pulled back into a pony tail and the shiny lip gloss made Eugene want to kiss her right then. When Cookie saw the giant teddy bear sitting next to him, her eyes got wide.

"Is that for me?" She asked with a big smile.

"Of course it is. He's to protect you and keep you company on the nights you're here alone."

"That's so sweet... Thank you," she said giving him a wet kiss.

She looked a little closer and noticed a gold necklace with a heart shaped charm, around the bear's neck. She removed it and held it in her hands as she gazed at it in amazement. Eugene took it from her and put it around her neck.

 "What did I do to deserve this?" She asked.

 "I'm really feeling you and I want you to know how special you are." Cookie blushed.

 "Thank you so much. You make me feel special."

They shared a passionate kiss and almost finished what they started in the bathroom, when they were interrupted by the doorbell. Cookie answered it and was taken by surprise when she opened it and was greeted by 2 dozen long stem roses. She turned around with tears in her eyes.

"Thank you, Mr. Robinson. This is too much. First, jewelry and now roses. I must really be special."

Eugene sat on the couch with his arms folded.

"Don't thank me, because I didn't send them." He said with a hint of attitude.

"If it wasn't you, then who sent them?" Cookie looked at the card and her heart sank as she read it.

"Roses are red, violets are blue
I love you so much I don't know what to do
P.S. Sorry about the window, I'll pay for it.
Love Sam"

"I can't believe him," Cookie yelled, marching to the kitchen to throw the flowers in the trash.

"Who are they from?" Eugene asked.

"My crazy ex-boyfriend. I told you he was insane. One day he breaks my window, the next day he sends me roses. He has two different personalities." Eugene hugged her tight and told her not to worry about it.

They gathered the food and went outside to start their picnic. Eugene spread the blanket on the grass, while Cookie laid the food out. She had roast beef sandwiches, macaroni salad, potato chips, shrimp cocktail and chocolate covered strawberries. They ate the sandwiches and fed each other shrimp.

"So, are you gonna tell me what happened to your eye?" Cookie asked dipping a shrimp in the cocktail sauce.

"Well when I left here last night, I got about 10 minutes away, and my two front tires came off. I lost control and ran into a pole, banging my head on the steering wheel. It's only a little cut."

"What? You mean your tires came off while you were driving?"

"Yeah pretty much." Eugene stated calmly.

"How did that happen?"

"I think it happened with a crow bar loosening up my lug nuts." Cookies jaw dropped as she put two and two together and realized that Sam was behind it.

"I'm sorry, Eugene. My ex has gone too far. I'm going to call the police and file a report."

"Don't stress it. You told me from the start what I was stepping into. Plus, I'm in too deep to turn around now. So if, or when, your ex brings another problem to my door step, I will handle it myself."

"I understand where you're coming from, but he is my problem, and I don't want you involved in my B.S so--"

"So nothing... Your problem is my problem and we'll take care of it together. Now fill me in on him and let me know what I'm working with." Eugene said. Cookie let out a relieved sigh.

"Ok. We met after I graduated from high school. Like all men, he was cool for the first few months, but then he got real possessive, always questioning my whereabouts and checking my cell phone. I thought he was just the jealous type, until his jealousy turned into fits of rage. It was scary because he would get angry and start yelling, and breaking things. But he never hit me. Not even once. I found out that he was bi-polar and that's why he acted the way he did. Both of his parents left him. Pretty much everybody in his corner turned their backs on him. This made it harder for me to leave him. Anyway we dated for about 3 years until he got locked up."

"What did he do to get arrested?" Eugene asked.

"He caught an attempted murder charge, but he pleaded down to aggravated assault." Cookie said softly.

"Wow that's crazy. What happened?"

"While I was in college, I was having a study lunch with one of my classmates. My boyfriend came up to the school to surprise me, but when he saw me and the other guy at the table together, he lost it. He beat the poor guy so bad, that he had to have reconstructive surgery on his face to repair the wounds. He was my girl Carol's boyfriend at the time. That's how we met. Thank GOD, he survived, but they gave my ex 5 years." She took a measured breath to calm herself before continuing.

"He wrote me and I wrote back for the first 6 months, but he was always accusing me of messing around on him, so I stopped visiting and writing. He kept sending me letters for his first 3 years. I never opened them or responded so he stopped writing. I didn't hear from him again until he showed up at my front door a few weeks ago."

"Well he better hope that our paths don't cross because I owe him an ass whipping for messing up my car." Eugene said, meaning every word.

"Once again, I'm sorry for the trouble he's caused. I will pay for all the damages."

"Don't sweat it baby. Everything's being taken care of. I'm driving my wife's car for now, so it's cool."

"Oh, that's her 300m outside?"

"Yeah that was an anniversary present last year."

"So, do you have to pick her up from work or something?" Cookie asked.

"Nah, she's driving the family van. Of course, she told me to drive the van and let her keep her car, but the 300 was blocking the van and I had to leave before her, so I hopped in her car and left," Eugene said laughing.

"You're something else... Tell me about your wife and kids."

"What do you want to know?"

"I want to know how you and your wife's relationship is. Tell me what your kids are like. You rarely talk about your family."

"That's because I don't want to make you feel uncomfortable by talking about them. But, as you know I have 2 kids, Thomas and Gina. My wife's name is Linda. We've been married for 6 years. Our marriage started off great until I had an affair two years ago the affair lasted for about ten months and when my wife found out, we separated for a while. We actually just got back on track two months ago."

"And look at me lil' Miss Helen Homewrecker," Cookie said. Eugene grinned ruefully,

"I don't know about all that. It takes two to tango, and I blame myself because I couldn't resist you. There was something about Cookie I had to have. Speaking of Cookie. How did you get that name?"

"My mom told me that I ate cookies so much that cookie was my first word. So she's been calling me that since I was 2. That's how I got the name. Not to mention that I'm sweet and I taste good." Cookie said with a seductive smile.

"You got that right. You taste like a slice of heaven. As a matter of fact I have a sweet tooth right now." Eugene said kissing her neck. Cookie giggled and fed him a strawberry. He pushed all the leftover food to the side and laid her down. He began to take off her pants, but she resisted.

"Boy, is you crazy. It's the middle of the day; what if somebody sees us?" She said with concern.

"It's cool if they see us, but if they stare and watch, then we need to charge them," he replied.

Eugene continued to pull on her sweat pants until they were off. He smiled when he noticed that she didn't have on any panties. He grabbed a strawberry and gently rubbed it across her clit. The coldness of the chocolate made her arch her back. He bit half the strawberry and fed the rest to her. Then he took another one and placed it slightly inside her. Just enough to get her wetness on the tip of the fruit. Eugene licked his lips after eating that strawberry in one bite. He started to taste her again but Cookie grabbed his hand and pulled him towards her.

"I want you inside of me," she whispered, no longer worried about being outside in her backyard in broad daylight. Eugene pulled his slacks down and slowly slid inside of her.

*   *   *

Linda was at work when she realized she left some important legal documents in the trunk of her car. On her lunch break she decided to go to Eugene's job to get the paper work out her car. When she pulled into the parking lot, she didn't see the car.

Maybe it's in the back, she thought as she got out of the minivan and went inside the bank.

"Hey Donna, can you get Eugene for me," Linda asked politely.

"Hi Linda, I'm sorry but Mr. Robinson left early for the day."

"Did he take an early lunch? How long has he been gone?" She asked, obviously in a rush.

"Actually he left around 10:30. He said he got into a car accident last night and he wasn't feeling to well, so he left for the day." Donna told her. Linda walked out with an attitude. She sat in the van and called Eugene's cell phone.

"Hey baby, I left some important papers in the trunk of my car. I came to your job to get them but they said you weren't feeling good, so you left early. If you get this message in time, please call me back. I hope you're ok. I love you. Bye."

Linda hung up and called the house phone, thinking he might have gone home, but no one answered. She thought he might be sleeping so she quickly drove to their house. When she got there her car wasn't in the driveway so she kept going and headed back to work, wondering what was going on with her husband.

First he's coming home late and hanging out with his boys more. Now he's nowhere to be found. I don't know what's going on but I don't like it, she thought to herself.

*   *   *

After moving the party from the back yard to the bedroom, Cookie and Eugene were laid out in the bed, both covered in sweat and out of breath.

"Eugene, what are you trying to do to me?" She asked.

"Make you feel as good as you make me feel." Before Cookie could respond, Eugene's cell phone rang. He got up and looked at the caller Id. He saw that it was his wife, but he didn't answer it. She left a message, so he checked it.

"Damn." He blurted out after listening to the voice mail she left him.

"What's the matter baby?" Cookie asked, beginning to fall asleep.

"Linda went to my job, because she left something in the trunk of her car." Cookie sat up with a worried look.

"What are we going to do?"

"We?" Eugene laughed. "You, are gonna get some rest. I, am going home and I'll call her on the way there."

"Okay," she said sadly.

"Don't be upset with me. I'll make it up to you."

"I'm not upset. It's just reality is setting in. I am really starting to fall for you and I realize that we'll never be more then what we have now." Eugene didn't know what to say. He just sat on the bed and held her tight.

"What do you want me to do baby?"

"There's nothing you can do. I have to not let my feelings get involved and take what we have for what it is and nothing more."

He rocked her in his arms until she fell asleep. Then he got dressed and made his way to the front door. As he was getting ready to leave, he spotted the card that came with the flowers. Eugene picked it up and read it. He then went to the kitchen and grabbed the roses out the trash can and left a note for Cookie.

'I got the flowers out of the garbage.
I hope you don't mind.
I figured you didn't want them
and I might need them because
I'm probably going to be in hot
water with the wife. So I'm just
re-gifting them. Lol.
I'll call you tonight and thanks for a
lovely day.
Eugene'

CHAPTER 8

The next day Cookie went to work with a smile. She and Carol were in the teachers' lounge eating bagels and drinking orange juice. Cookie was telling her about the lust filled day off she had.

"What?! He sucked a strawberry out of you. That man is a freak. And you're a freak for letting him do it." Carol said, laughing and slapping five with Cookie. They continued to joke and laugh until Tony walked in the room with a swollen lip and stitches in his head. Cookie stood up and rushed to his side.

"What happened to you, Tony?" She asked touching his face. He smacked her hand away and took a step back.

"What happened? Psycho Sam happened. Your crazy boyfriend attacked me outside in the parking lot. He threatened me with a gun and told me to leave you alone. As a matter of fact, I'm not even supposed to be talking to you right now." Tony yelled, causing the other teachers in the lounge to stare at him. Cookie was in shock and didn't know what to say.

"I'm sorry, Tony. The other night, he busted my window with a crow bar. He is totally out of control and I don't know what to do."

"I know what I'm going to do. I'm leaving you the hell alone. Your head is good, but it's not worth getting killed over." Tony spat coldly. Cookie was hurt and embarrassed by his harsh words. His eyes were starting to water, but before she could respond, Carol was all over him.

"I know you are not coming at my girl like it's her fault. You limp dick, sorry excuse for a man. Sitting here tryna play her, when you can't even keep it up." Carol yelled in his face.

Tony's face turned beet red. He looked at Cookie, then at Carol, who was smiling.

He felt humiliated, because of what Carol said in front of everyone. Out of anger, he smacked her so hard that her earring flew across the room. She recovered quickly and kicked him in his privates. Tony doubled over in pain and she kneed him in the face, causing him to fall backwards.

"You cotton picking moulie. I'll kill you!" He yelled from the ground with blood leaking out of his mouth. "I've had it with your crap. Get out of here. You're fired!!"

"You don't have the authority to fire me, but it don't matter, because I quit." Carol shot back.

"Good, but this ain't the last you'll see of me." Tony said with venom in his voice.

Carol walked out of the lounge and left. She thought about calling the police and filing charges, but she decided to let her boyfriend Nigel handle it. Cookie looked at Tony and shook her head.

"What?? You can quit also, I could care less. I don't need you or your crazy boyfriend stressing me out. I'm back with my wife anyway, so who needs you." He said brushing himself off. Cookie glared at him through squinted eyes.

"I can't believe you Tony, and no I'm not quitting, just because you're an asshole. But if you ever disrespect me again, I will make sure Psycho Sam does more than threaten you." Cookie said, pushing past Tony to catch up with Carol.

*   *   *

It was a little past 10 pm and Carol was on the phone with Nigel, telling him what took place between her and Tony.

"Yeah baby, he lost his mind, putting his hands on me. But I got him good. I did just like you taught me. You should've seen it. I must admit though, I am pissed that I lost my job and I--" Carol stopped mid-sentence because of the doorbell ringing.

"Hold on baby, somebody's at the door." Carol said, getting off the couch and looking through the peep hole. The person had their back to her and she couldn't tell who it was. Carol dropped the phone when the person turned around. "W-W-What are you doing here?" She stammered nervously.

"You know why I'm here." He replied, grabbing her by the throat and shoving her into the house. She stumbled and fell backwards as he shut the door.

"What do you want? Why are you doing this?" She cried.

He didn't respond, he just took her by the hair and dragged her into the kitchen. Carol kicked and screamed, trying to get away. The intruder began to lose his grip on her hair so he kicked her in the face, causing her to lose consciousness as well as a few teeth.

Carol was awakened by the sharp pain of something thrusting inside of her. When she opened her eyes she realized she was being raped. She screamed and tried to push him away, but he was too heavy. He covered her mouth with his hand and she bit his finger. He yelled and pulled his hand back. She used that opportunity to scratch his face. She was going for the eyes, but got his cheek instead. He put his massive hands around her neck and slowly squeezed the life out of Carol, while he continued to ram his manhood inside of her.

After he finished, he stood up and kicked her lifeless body. A devilish grin spread across his face as he thought, *I always wanted to know how her sex game was... A little too dry for me, but she does like it rough so I give her an 'A' in my book.* He blew her lifeless body a kiss and quickly left.

*   *   *

It was 3 o'clock in the morning when Cookie was awoken by the sound of her cell phone ringing. She answered groggily, but was instantly jarred awake by the news of Carol's death.

"Nigel, tell me what happen. How did she die?" Cookie asked, tears welling up instantly in her eyes.

"We were on the phone talking and she was telling me about what went down between her and Tony. She told me to hold on because it was someone at the door. Next thing I know the phone hung up. I tried calling back, but I kept getting the busy signal. I didn't know what happened, but I didn't think much of it. I got off work at 12am, and when I walked through the door, I knew something was wrong. The front door was unlocked, and the cordless phone was broken on the floor." Nigel paused for a second to gather himself.

"I called her name and searched all over the house... I-I-I found her in the kitchen... She was beat and raped, Cookie... The bastard murdered my baby." Nigel said, his voice cracking as he broke down. Cookie cried also, but she knew she had to be strong for Nigel. They talked for a little while longer and Cookie offered to take care of the funeral arrangements while Nigel contacted Carol's family.

"Cookie do you have any idea who would want to hurt Carol?" Nigel asked with desperation.

"No, you know as well as I do Nigel, she was loved by everyone. The only person I could think of that might have anything against her is Tony. They really didn't care for each other."

"Tony? Do you mean the principal she got into it with?"

"Yeah." Cookie replied.

"I'm gonna kill him." Nigel yelled.

"Don't do anything to get yourself in trouble."

"Cookie, I gotta go. I'll talk to you later." He quickly said before hanging up.

Cookie cradled the pillow close to her chest and cried herself to sleep.

*   *   *

A week after Carol's funeral, Cookie was still grieving.

Eugene had been there for her every step of the way, comforting her and showing his support. They became a lot closer, and the more time he spent with Cookie, the less time he spent with his wife and kids. Linda knew something was up with her husband, but he denied it every time she asked him about it.

"Eugene, I tell you I'm not going through this again. If you're having another affair, just let me know, and I'll be on my way."

"Linda, how many times do I have to tell you that I'm not cheating on you? Stop judging me based off my past mistakes. I thought we were trying to work through all that." Eugene replied.

"I thought we were also, but lately you haven't been the same. You're always working late and all of a sudden you have to take business trips out of town. Did you forget I heard all of the same B-S a year ago, when you were having an affair. I swear if I leave you this time, me and the kids are gone for good." Linda said with tears in her eyes.

Eugene grabbed his wife and hugged her tight. He kissed her softly on the forehead and gently wiped her tears away.

*   *   *

Cookie finally pulled herself together and went back to work. She'd been out for two weeks, and when she walked in the school, all the teachers came up to her to offer their deepest condolences. Even though it was hard, she made it through the day without breaking down. That was, until Tony walked into her classroom.

"Hey, Miss Taylor. How are you holding up?" Cookie just stared at him with a blank look.

"What do you want Tony?" She replied with ice in her voice.

"I just came to check on you. I'm sorry about your loss. I know how close you and Carol were."

"How can you be sorry when you're the one who killed her, you sick bastard." Tony closed the door and stepped towards Cookie. She back pedaled until her back was against the chalk board.

"What the hell are you talking about? It's a fact that Carol and I had our problems, but I did not rape and kill her." Tony said convincingly.

"Who said anything about her being raped?"

"I-I-I seen it on the news that she was sexually assaulted and--"

"Stay away from me Tony. I can't believe you would do something like that. Right now, I don't have any proof, but I'm going to the police anyway." Cookie yelled.

Tony stepped so close to her that she could smell the turkey sandwich he had for lunch on his breath.

"I don't care what you *think* I did, but I didn't have anything to do with Carol's death. And if you even look at a police officer, you'll regret it. So keep your thoughts and feelings to yourself. And if you *think* I'm playing just *think* about what happened to your friend." Tony said with fire in his eyes. He turned around and left the classroom, leaving Cookie scared out of her mind.

Right then and there, she decided that it would be her last year teaching at MLK Elementary. At the end of the year she would transfer to Hill Crest Elementary. *I only have a couple of months left until I no longer have to deal with Tony again,* Cookie thought to herself.

CHAPTER 9

Cookie made it through the rest of the week, without any run-ins with Tony. And once she thought about it, she hadn't seen him since their last encounter in her classroom. On Saturday, she decided to leave the house to get her hair and nails done. Eugene was supposed to be taking her to the comedy club later on and she wanted to look her best. After getting her nails done, Cookie walked into Unique's Hair and Spa Treatment. As always, it was jam packed.

"Hey 'Nique." Cookie said as she entered the shop. Unique looked up and stopped doing her clients hair, as she rushed over to give Cookie a hug.

"How are you doing Cookie? I'm sorry to hear about your loss. I know you and Carol was like sisters. Everyone here at the shop loved her too. Carol will truly be missed," Unique said sincerely.

"Thanks girl. Her untimely death crushed me, but I'm tryna stay strong."

"Well just remember we are all here for you. As a matter of fact, I can squeeze you in next if you want."

"Thanks I appreciate it, but I'm gonna let Sabria hook me up." Cookie said with a smile.

"Okay that's cool. I'm sure she can use the business. Anyway, remember what I said. If you need ANYTHING, you just let me know."

"Thanks, 'Nique," Cookie said giving her another hug. Cookie sat around gossiping and laughing with the other girls in the shop. It felt good to smile and let loose again.

*　　*　　*

"Girl, you wanna talk about a man with a good stroke game... I'm messing with this guy that is a certified pipe layer. And on top of that he has a tongue like a rattle snake," Cookie said laughing and slapping five with another girl.

"Is Mr. Pipe Layer married? Because we all know how you get down," Unique yelled from the front of the shop.

"You know he is. That's the best way to have them, because when I'm done with them, I can send them back to their wives. No strings attached."

"Cookie, you ain't no good!" Another girl said laughing.

"Tell that to my new boy toy. He says I have the best cookies in the world. Besides if his wife was taking care of business, then I wouldn't have to," Cookie replied. Most of the girls were laughing, and giving high fives to each other. But, there were a few married women in the shop who didn't find anything funny, and Linda was one of them. She glared at Cookie with animosity, and Cookie didn't even notice the cold stares coming from

Linda's way. Cookie finally sat in the chair to get her hair done, and she was still bragging about her new man.

"Does he have a job?" Sabria asked.

"Of course, he works at a bank."

"Oh yeah... Which one?"

"Like I'm gonna tell you, so that you can go get him." Cookie said laughing.

"Well see if he has a brother, cousin, a friend or something. I need a plumber that knows how to lay pipe. Because the plumber I got has rusty tools," Sabria joked, causing everyone in the shop to burst out laughing.

*   *   *

Later on that night Cookie and Eugene were on their way to the comedy club. Eugene seemed quiet and distant.

"What's the matter baby?" Cookie asked.

"It's that obvious huh?"

"Yeah, so what's going on?"

"I'm sorry, Linda and I got into a fight before I left the house. Everything was all good earlier today, but she came home with an attitude and started accusing me of cheating... We had a big argument and once again she threatened to divorce me and take my kids. So my mind isn't all here right now."

"I'm sorry to hear that. Why don't we just turn around and go back to my house. You can drop me off, so you can go home and make things right with your wife," Cookie told him sincerely.

"Thanks for being so supportive and understanding, but we both need to go out and have a good time, just to take our minds off the madness." Cookie was silent for a while before she spoke again.

"Maybe we should take a break from seeing each other. I really don't want to come in between you and your family." Cookie said softly.

"To be honest, Cookie, I already gave it some thought. But I couldn't leave you alone, even if I wanted to. I'm in love with you." Cookie was speechless. That was the first time he had expressed his love for her, and truth be told, she felt the same way.

"I love you too baby, and that's the problem." She replied.

"What is?" Eugene asked.

"I'm in love with a married man."

They rode in silence for the rest of the ride. Both lost in their own thoughts. When they got to the comedy club, everything was momentarily back in order. They laughed, ate, drank, and had a good time.

*   *   *

Linda was calling Eugene's cell phone, but he turned it off, so she kept getting the voice mail. Out of frustration she threw the phone against the wall, breaking it into pieces. Even though she didn't have proof of her husband's infidelity, women's intuition told her that he was being unfaithful. Linda loved Eugene and she wanted to give him the benefit of the doubt. She didn't want to lose her husband, so while lying in bed she decided to fight for her marriage. She would try her best to keep her man, but if he didn't want to be kept, then it was out of her hands.

*   *   *

Halfway back to Cookie's house, they became quiet again as guilt started to settle in. They pulled into the driveway and just sat there. Neither one moving nor speaking. Eugene finally broke the awkward silence.

"Sooo, where do we go from here?" He asked.

"I go inside to my empty house and you go back home to your wife and kids." She replied sarcastically.

"Come on now. No need to be rude."

"I'm not being rude, I'm being real."

"Once again, I ask you what do *you* want me to do." Eugene said slightly raising his voice.

"Ask yourself that question. What do *you* want to do Mr. Robinson? Huh?"

"I don't know what I want to do, but I know what I *don't* want to do... And that's lose you. Cookie, you have opened a door in my heart I never knew existed. Of course I wish I could have my cake and eat it too, but that's not gonna happen. Baby, I'm stuck between a rock and a hard place and I don't know what to do."

"Well, I know what I want, but I can't ask you to leave your family for me. That's a choice you have to make on your own."

"But I can't make that choice." Eugene said softly.

"Then let me help you." Cookie said. And with that she got out of the car and went inside her house, never once looking back. She wanted him to get out the car and follow her, but he didn't. Eugene opened his mouth to speak, but no words came out. He wanted to knock on her door, but his legs wouldn't move. So he just sat in the car with his head on the steering wheel.

*   *   *

Cookie was sitting on the couch, crying with her head in her hands. Max could sense something was wrong. He nudged his tiny wet nose against her leg and she scooped him up into a cuddle.

A few minutes later, Cookie was startled by a knock on the door. She wiped her eyes and smiled as she thought Eugene decided to choose her after all. Cookie swung the door open with excitement and was prepared to jump into her lover's arms. Her look of joy turned into disappointment as she locked eyes with Sam.

"Hey, baby." He said, walking past her and making himself comfortable on the couch. Cookie looked outside for any sign of Eugene. She didn't see him, so she closed the door and rolled her eyes, wondering what Sam wanted.

"Why are you here Sam?" Cookie asked with her hands on her hips.

"I haven't talked to you in a while. The last time I seen you... You were... Well, you know. And that reminds me... Here. This is for the cost of the window." He said, holding out 5 crisp 100 dollar bills.

"Sam, you know I don't need your money."

"Oh yeah, I forgot, the only child of a doctor and an engineer. Your parents died in a plane crash on the way back from their vacation, and left you a load of money. Lucky you!"

"You call losing both of my parent's luck? Just because I inherited a few dollars... I would give up every penny, to have them back!" Cookie shouted. Sam stood up to hug her.

"I'm sorry, baby, I didn't mean to upset you. Let's forget about it. I just came here to pay for the window and tell you something."

"I don't need your money. What I need is for you to get it through your head, that what we had is over. You're stalking my house, messing up Tony's car. And you beat him up. If that ain't enough, you throw a crow bar through my window, *AFTER* you unscrewed the lug nuts on my friend's car. When is the madness gonna stop?"

"When you realize that we should be together."

"Sam, I think it's time for you to go, and if you don't, I'll be forced to call the police." Cookie threatened.

"If you even think about calling the police, I'll kill your little boyfriend, Eugene." Sam shot back. Cookie's eyes widened.

"Oh yeah, I know all about your new boy toy. I also know that he's married with 2 kids and he lives in a big house, just outside of town. First, Tony, and now Eugene. You must really have a thing for married men." Sam said with a smile.

"GET OUT RIGHT NOW!!" Cookie screamed. Sam spread his hands defensively.

"Okay, fine, I'm leaving... But I'll be back. And I want you to know something... If I ever catch Eugene over here again... I. Will. Kill. Him. As a matter of fact, I'll kill his family first. I advise you to call him and tell him that it's over. I'm not playing. If I see y'all two together again, I'm driving straight to his house to have a talk with Linda and the kids." Sam said as he walked out laughing. Cookie locked the door and slid to the floor crying.

CHAPTER 10

A few weeks passed and Eugene had been calling Cookie every day, but she never answered. He would leave messages, begging her to call him back. And as bad as she wanted to, she didn't, out of fear that Psycho Sam would stay true to his word. A few times Eugene even showed up at her house, but Cookie refused to open the door. Eventually, he got the hint and concentrated on making his marriage work. Psycho Sam would show up at her job with lunch, so Cookie had no choice but to see him when he popped up like that.

One day, she left work late, and decided to have a few drinks at the bar. By the time she got home, Sam was sitting on her front step.

"Where have you been?" He demanded, before she could even get out the car.

"What?"

"You heard me. I've been out here waiting for you for almost 2 hours. You should've been home."

"I don't know what your problem is, but you better get out of my face with all that Psycho drama," Cookie spat angrily.

"I know where you were at. You were out with Eugene. I wasn't joking when I told you to stay away from him."

"First of all, I wasn't with him. We haven't seen each other since you threatened to hurt his family. And second, you are *not* my man, so don't be keeping tabs on me. True indeed, you bring me lunch sometimes, but don't get it twisted. We Are *NOT* together." Sam's face suddenly softened.

"I'm sorry baby. You know how I get when it comes to you. I brought over some movies. I thought we could order some pizza and chill," Sam said with puppy dog eyes. Cookie looked at him and smiled in spite of herself. Sam got on her nerves a lot, but there were times when he could make her melt with his almond brown eyes that complimented his light skin complexion. Sam always had a nice body, but the five years in prison had added more muscle to his already built frame. Cookie walked in the house with Sam on her heels. He quickly got comfortable on the couch, and played with Max while Cookie changed her clothes.

After a quick shower, she made her way downstairs and found Sam watching sports center. A few minutes later, Papa Johns was delivering a large cheese pizza. They sat on the sofa with Max in between them, watching the latest Saw movie.

*   *   *

When Cookie got up use the bathroom, Sam crushed up two ecstasy pills and slipped them in her soda. He had been trying to get Cookie to sleep with him ever since he got out of jail. But she was being stingy with her cookies and he was determined to get some, even if he had to take them.

After the movie went off, Sam made his move. He pulled Cookie towards him and tried to kiss her, but she turned her head.

"Slow your roll, buddy. I told you that it isn't that type of party. Thanks for the movie and pizza but I think it's time to call it a night," Cookie said politely. Sam stared in her eyes and licked his lips. Something came over Cookie and she got the sudden urge to push Sam down on the floor and ride his face. The E-pills were starting to kick in and he could tell by the look in her eyes that she was feeling it.

He used his finger tips to slowly caress her arms. Cookie closed her eyes and shuddered with pleasure, wondering why his touch suddenly felt so good.

Sam could feel the goose bumps on her arms, so he took that as an invitation to take it a step further. He moved closer and planted wet kisses on her neck. Her mouth was quietly saying no, but her mind and body was screaming yes. Sam smoothly took off her shirt and was pleasantly surprised to see that she wasn't wearing a bra. He quickly latched onto her right breast like a hungry new born baby. Cookie arched her back and regretfully let out a soft moan.

What am I doing? She thought. *It's wrong, but it feels so good. Oh well... I haven't had sex in a while, and this one time won't hurt.* She reasoned with herself.

Sam slid down Cookie's sweat pants, while she lifted up to make it easier. He slid her panties to the side and tasted her sweet nectar. Cookie screamed, feeling like her entire body was on fire and his tongue was the only thing that could put out the flames. She grabbed him by the head and ground her pelvis into his face. Sam greedily drank every drop and stood up with an accomplished smile.

He positioned himself to enter her, but she placed her hands on his chest, stopping him in his tracks.

 "No Sam, I don't think we should do this," Cookie said weakly. Sam had to bite his tongue, to refrain from cursing her out. In one swift motion, he ripped her panties off; Cookie was surprised and felt herself being turned on by his aggressiveness. Sam rubbed the head of his shaft on her clit. Cookie spread her legs, giving him easier access. She scooted closer, so he could penetrate her, but he teased her.

 "Put it in." She quietly begged. That was just what he wanted to hear. He braced himself and slowly entered her. She was so tight and wet that Sam almost came upon entry. It had been a long time since he last had sex with Cookie, and he took his time, enjoying each stroke.

She couldn't believe that it felt so good. Sam wasn't as big as Eugene, but for some reason, she was experiencing the best sex of her life. Cookie put her arms around his neck and lifted up, so he could go deeper. She screamed as she reached her second orgasm.

Turned on by the faces and loud moans she made, Sam increased his rhythm and stroked harder. Cookie grabbed her breast and gently pinched her nipples.

They went at it for two hours, switching positions and pleasing each other, until they fell asleep on the living room floor.

Cookie woke up around 3am. Her mouth felt like sand paper and she had a queasy feeling in her stomach. She looked around and realized she was in the living room. When Cookie looked over at Sam still sleeping, the memories of everything that had happened came flooding back to her. *What did I get myself into?* She asked herself.

Cookie went upstairs and took a shower. The water ran down her face and mixed in with the tears that were falling. Cookie wanted to be happy with a man of her own, not somebody else's husband that she borrowed from time to time. She got out and dried off. When she opened the door, Sam was standing there with a crazed look on his face.

"What were you doing?" He asked.

"I was taking a shower. What do you think I was doing?" She said brushing by him, with an attitude.

"What's wrong with you? Did I do something wrong?" He asked with a puzzled look.

"No, you didn't do anything wrong, but I did."

"Come on baby, talk to me."

"Sam. I think you should just leave."

"I'm not going anywhere until you talk to me." Sam yelled louder than he meant to.

"WILL YOU PLEASE GET OUT...? I need time to think."

Sam saw the fury in her eyes and decided to let it go. Even though he wanted to know what made her switch up on him. Without saying another word, he turned and left, slamming the door behind him.

Miserable and confused, Cookie picked up the phone and started to call Carol, but she stopped mid-dial when she realized Carol was not going to answer. She put the phone back down, and cried herself to sleep.

*   *   *

Cookie was startled by a loud banging on the door. She slowly got up to answer it. She looked out the peep hole, but it was too dark to see who it was. She opened the door and Tony rushed in with a gun. He had the look of death in his eyes. He didn't speak one word. He just aimed the gun at her chest and fired twice...

Cookie jumped up, screaming, and feeling for blood on her chest. She wiped the sweat off her head and thanked GOD it was only a dream.

CHAPTER 11

Eugene hadn't seen or talked to Cookie in over a month. He missed her dearly, but he knew she was a fling that he had to let go. And he put more effort into spending time with his family. Linda started dressing sexier and showing him more attention and she thought that's why he had changed his ways.

After a long night of passionate love making, they both laid in the bed while the alarm clock was going off. Neither one of them tried to move.

"It's time to wake up Baby." Linda said rubbing his chest. Eugene looked at the clock as the red 6:00am flashed on and off. He wished he could lie in bed all day.

"Hit the snooze button for me, sweetheart... Just give me a couple more minutes."

"Come on. We both have busy days ahead of us. And don't forget that we have the parent/teacher conference at MLK Elementary." Linda said.

Eugene quickly got up at the thought of seeing Cookie again. Just thinking about having sex with her had him hard as a rock. Linda noticed his erection and smiled to herself. Eugene stood up to stretch and Linda pushed him back on the bed. Before he could say anything, she took him into her mouth. His morning stiffness and her warm tongue, made a perfect combination. His loud grunts caused Linda to put her all into it.

After pleasing him for ten minutes, Eugene came with such force, that it made Linda choke as it shot down her throat. He stood up to return the favor, but she declined.

"That's ok. My cookies are still sore from last night. I just broke you off, so you could get your day started on a good note." Linda smiled.

"Baby, that was good enough to get my whole week started on a good note."

"Anything for you, Honey." Linda said, glad to have her husband back.

*   *   *

Around 7pm, Eugene pulled into the school parking lot. He had butterflies in his stomach, because he was anxious to see Cookie. He didn't know if he would run into her or not. Eugene had no idea who his kids' teachers were, but he secretly prayed that they would at least get a chance to talk to Cookie for a minute. He purposely dressed for the occasion. Eugene had on his Steve Harvey collection suit, with the shoes to match. He waited in the parking lot, until his wife and two kids showed up. He got out of the car and helped Linda with the children. His daughter Gina ran to him and jumped in his arms. He playfully tickled her.

"How's Daddy's little girl?"

"I'm fine... Look at what I made for you." She said holding out a picture she had drawn.

"Thank you princess. I'm gonna hang this on the wall in my office." Eugene and his family walked into the school.

The anxiety was starting to show. Linda noticed, but thought nothing of it. First they went to Gina's kindergarten class, where she showed her parents all of her art work, along with the class pet hamster, whose name was Lucky. Gina's teacher Mrs. Wilson talked to Linda, while Gina gave her Dad a tour of her classroom.

Afterwards, they went to talk to Thomas' teachers starting with his homeroom. As they walked by different classrooms, Eugene looked into each one, hoping to catch a glimpse of Cookie.

"Hello, I'm Mr. Dixon. Thanks for coming. Please feel free to walk around and check things out. If you have any questions, I'll be happy to answer them."

"Thank you, Mr. Dixon. I would like to know how my son's behavior is. I have received calls from the principal and other teachers about Thomas acting up, but I've yet to hear from you." Linda said.

"To be quite frank, Thomas is a good kid. He has a lot of energy and should learn how to channel all that energy in a positive way. He does have a problem with talking when he shouldn't, but overall he is a good boy." Mr. Dixon said ruffling Thomas' hair.

Linda looked at the list in her hand. It had the classroom number, teachers name and subject. They had already seen two of his teachers and Linda was glad that his math teacher was the last one. When they walked into Miss Taylor's classroom, Eugene's heart fell to the pit of his stomach. Cookie was talking to another parent with her back to him. The tight fitting navy blue skirt she had on, hugged her frame just right. When Cookie turned around and saw Eugene, she stopped her words mid-sentence. Cookie quickly wrapped things up with the parents she was speaking to, and turned her attention towards Eugene and his family.

 "Hello, Miss Taylor. My name is Linda and this is my husband Eugene. We are Thomas' parents," Linda said proudly. Cookie smiled and shook their hands, but she held onto Eugene's hand a little longer than she should have.

Linda noticed the exchange and her suspicions were renewed. As she studied Cookie, Linda thought she looked familiar, but she couldn't remember where she knew her from. Linda knew her face and voice from somewhere, but she couldn't put her finger on it.

Eugene sat back while the two ladies talked about his son's schoolwork and behavior. Cookie would cut her eyes at Eugene when she thought Linda wasn't looking, but Linda noticed the nervousness in her husband's face. Cookie was telling Linda about Thomas' grades, but Linda wasn't listening. Her mind was on figuring out why Eugene was acting so strange, and where she knew Miss Taylor from.

"Will you excuse me for a second," Linda said walking towards her husband.

Cookie couldn't hear what was being said, but she could tell by Linda's body language, that she was upset about something. When Eugene held out his arms and hugged his wife, Cookie felt a twinge of jealousy. But when the two shared a passionate kiss, Cookie's knees buckled, and she had to catch herself from falling. Eugene kissed his wife for two reasons.

For one, Linda was asking him questions about why he was looking at Miss Taylor that way. So he hugged and kissed her to put out the fire of an argument that was brewing. Linda melted in his arms and momentarily put the negative thoughts out of her mind.

Eugene also kissed Linda for Cookie's sake. He wanted to make her jealous, and just as he thought, Cookie was filled with envy, and it was written all over her face.

Linda went to wrap things up with Miss Taylor and Eugene walked out of the classroom without saying goodbye to Cookie. That sent her over the edge, but she played it cool.

Cookie sat at her desk in total shock. She couldn't believe that Eugene and Linda were the parents of little Tommy Mitchell. And she really couldn't believe how Eugene had played her. *I guess I deserve that, by the way I treated him. I should have answered his calls when he tried to reach me. I know he kissed his wife like that, just to get under my skin. But damn, he looked good. I didn't realize how much I miss him, until now.*

*　　*　　*

On the way back home, Linda was in deep thought. She was still trying to figure out where she knew Miss Taylor from.

Eugene was in a world of his own, as he followed his wife's car back to their home. He thought about making a U-turn and going back to see Cookie. He pulled out his cell phone to call her, but hesitated. While debating back and forth about if he should call her or not, his cell phone rang. Eugene looked at the caller id and saw that it was his wife calling. He took that as a sign.

"Hey baby. What's up?" He said, answering the phone.

"Eugene, I have to ask you something, and please be honest... Do you know Miss Taylor?"

"Who is Miss Taylor?" He asked, playing dumb.

"Miss Taylor is Tommy's math teacher. You know the one you were acting weird around," Linda spat. Eugene was quiet for a second as he thought of a lie. Linda took his silence as an indication that he knew her.

"Eugene, did you hear what I said?" Linda yelled.

"Yeah I heard you, but I don't know what makes you think I know her. I told you I didn't when you asked me that in the classroom."

"Then why were y'all two looking at each other like that?"

"Like what?" Eugene yelled, allowing the exasperation into his voice.

"Come on now Eugene. Please don't insult my intelligence. You know what I'm talking about." Linda replied calmly.

"You know, you're really starting to piss me off Linda. I'll talk to you when we get home." Eugene said, hanging up the phone.

He tried to think of a way to get out of the mess he was about to get into. *Maybe I will just throw it on her real good tonight and take her out for a romantic dinner tomorrow night. That should calm her down and take her mind off of this Miss Taylor business. I must admit. That was a close call*, he thought.

Eugene stopped by McDonalds and got his kids each a Happy Meal, even though Tommy didn't deserve anything, because of the report they had received from his teachers. He also got Linda a Big Mac meal and two hot apple pies. They were her favorite and he hoped it would help settle things down a little bit.

When he got home, they all ate at the table. Linda was quiet the whole time, and when Eugene talked to her, she only responded with one word answers. Eugene put the kids to bed, while Linda took a shower. He made dinner reservations for him and his wife for the following night at a popular restaurant called 'Mi Casa'. It was a fancy place and you had to have reservations in order to get a table.

In the shower, Linda got a chance to clear her head and think for a little bit.

I may have jumped to conclusions. I just got my husband back and I don't want my jealousy to drive him away. Lord knows that I love that man. But I know Miss Taylor from somewhere... I'm sure Eugene is upset with me because I have been giving him the silent treatment, but I'll just give him some tonight and he'll get over it, she thought as she rinsed the soap off of her body.

Eugene and Linda talked for a while, before having intense make up sex. Eugene closed his eyes and imagined he was making love to Cookie.

45 minutes later, Linda was asleep, and he was staring up at the ceiling, thinking about Cookie. He looked over at the alarm clock and it read quarter after twelve. He got out of bed and jumped in the shower.

As he washed up, the thought crossed his mind to call Cookie. He quickly got out of the shower, dried off and put on his jogging suit.

Instead of calling her, he decided to just go to her house.

He quietly grabbed his keys and left without waking up his wife. On the way to Cookie's house he got nervous about just showing up un-announced, so he went to call her on his cell phone. Eugene cursed himself, when he realized he had left his phone at home on the dresser.

He pulled into Cookie's driveway and thought about going back home, but the bulge growing in his pants, made him knock on the door. Cookie and Max were chilling on the couch when she heard a soft knock on the door. Her first thoughts were that it was Sam, and she started to ignore him, but she got up to answer it anyway. To her surprise, when she opened the door, Eugene was standing there with that sexy smile she loved.

Linda rolled over in the bed, reaching for her husband, but he wasn't there. She called his name, thinking he was in the bathroom. When he didn't answer, she got up and checked, but he wasn't in there. She looked in the kids' rooms before searching the rest of the house. Finally, she looked outside and noticed that his car was gone. Linda picked up the house phone and called his cell. She got upset when she heard it ringing upstairs in the bedroom.

*   *   *

"It's about time. I've been waiting to hear from you since you walked out of my classroom without even saying bye," Cookie said, standing in the doorway.

"Well, my wife kinda figured out something was going on between us and I had to smooth things over before I could talk to you."

"I could tell something was up, by the way she was all up in your face." Cookie said.

"Yeah, but it's all good now."

"I'm glad to hear that."

"Sooo... Are you gonna let me in or what?"

"I don't know, should I let you in?" Cookie asked with a smile. Eugene took a step forward and kissed her. They fell into the house and he kicked the door shut behind him.

Cookie playfully pushed Eugene and ran up the stairs, but half way up he grabbed her from behind and turned her around. He kissed her roughly, while they tore at each other's clothes. Cookie put her right foot on the step rail and put her left leg over his shoulder. Eugene slowly entered her and felt like it was no place better on earth. The carpet on the stairs was starting to give her back rug burn, so they switched positions and she put her hands and knees on the steps, while Eugene penetrated her from behind.

They pleased each other for another 20 minutes, before taking it to the bedroom. Eugene lay on his back while Cookie slid up and down on his shaft. She scratched his chest and screamed as he lifted his waist and pushed deeper in side of her.

*   *   *

Linda sat on the couch in complete darkness. No lights, no TV, no radio. Just the sound of the wall clock ticking.

She was deep in thought about her husband's whereabouts. She didn't know if he was still mad at her or if he had an emergency and left so fast that he forgot his cell phone. Linda went upstairs and retrieved the phone off the dresser. She checked it for recent incoming calls, but the last incoming call was from her cell phone. She checked the outgoing calls and the last call he made was also to her cell phone. Out of curiosity she scrolled through his phone book to see the list of names and numbers he had. As she went from name to name, she stopped when she saw the name Cookie.

Cookie... Cookie... Where do I know that name from? She thought. Then it hit her like a slap in the face. Cookie was the woman from the hair salon that was bragging about sleeping with married men. As she mentally placed a face with the name and voice, Linda dropped the phone, when she realized that Miss Taylor and Cookie were one in the same.

So that's why Eugene was acting so funny. I can't believe that he would lie to me about it. After all we've been through. I'm tired of trying to make this marriage work. This is the last straw.

Linda fell asleep with thoughts of divorce on her mind.

*   *   *

"Looks like we're back at square one." Eugene said putting on his pants.

"Yeah. Just when I thought I was over you."

"That makes one of us, because I couldn't get over you, but since you refused to see me, I had no choice but to stick it out with Linda. But, please believe that you have been on my mind every day," he said sincerely.

"I feel you, but like I said before, I'm in love with a married man. And it hurts that you'll never be mine."

"I understand, so what would you like me to do?"

"I don't know. Just call me tomorrow or something. We have to take this one day at a time." Cookie said softly.

Eugene gathered his stuff, kissed Cookie on the forehead and quietly left. When he got to his car, the doors were locked and his keys were still in the ignition. He knocked on Cookie's door, and a couple minutes later she answered with red eyes like she'd been crying.

"What's the matter baby?" He asked, noticing she was clearly upset.

"Nothing." She lied. "Did you forget something?"

"No, I just locked my keys in the car and I need to use your phone to call Pop-a-Lock." Eugene made the call to have his door opened.

While he waited, he and Cookie talked some more. She explained to him that she was lonely and she wanted to settle down, get married and start a family of her own. Eugene understood, and part of him thought about leaving his wife to begin a new life with Cookie. But he knew, deep down inside, that would never be possible.

When Pop-a-Lock arrived, they had his door open in no time. Eugene didn't have any cash on him, so Cookie paid the 60 dollar bill. He thanked her with a passionate kiss and drove home in deep thought. When he got home, his wife was still asleep...

Or so he thought.

CHAPTER 12

Cookie dragged her feet as she got ready for work. Thanks to Eugene, she had been up most of the night. Even after he left, she was still awake for a while.

Thank God it's Friday, Cookie thought as she grabbed her car keys and left the house. As she was unlocking her car door, Sam came up from behind her. It seemed like he appeared from nowhere. Cookie jumped when he gripped her arm.

"Natasha, we need to talk." Sam said with ice in his voice. Cookie was shocked to hear her first name being called. She turned around and stood face to face with her worst nightmare.

"Please not right now. Sam. I'm already running late. I don't have time to deal with your craziness."

"Don't worry I won't be long. I just came by to tell you something."

"Make it quick." She replied. Sam cracked a nasty grin and shook his head.

"Ok, first of all, I thought I told you to stay away from Eugene. You must think--"

"Save it because I don't want to hear it." Cookie said cutting him off. She tried to turn around and get in her car, but Sam grabbed her arm and pulled her closer to him.

"Check this out, Natasha. You will listen to what I have to say. I'm trying to be nice, but you're really testing my patience. So I advise you to shut your mouth, and open your ears, before I get mad. Do you understand?" Cookie saw death in his eyes and she could hear the seriousness in his voice, so she obediently nodded her head. He continued.

"Good. Now as I was saying, you must think I'm stupid or something. I told you to stay away from him, yet he comes over here in the middle of the night. But I won't take it out on you. I told you what would happen if y'all two were still sleeping with each other."

"Sam, why can't you get over the fact that we're through. You don't have to hurt innocent people." Cookie pleaded.

"You're right, I don't *have* to hurt innocent people... But I *will*, and it's all *your* fault. But the worst part is that he's married. First Tony, now Eugene. Who down with OPP? Cookie down with OPP." Sam said laughing. She didn't reply, Cookie just glared at him with venom in her eyes.

"Don't worry, you'll be able to have him all to yourself, after I kill his pretty wife. Linda. I haven't decided if I'm gonna kill the kids or not. Who knows, I might just kill them for the hell of it."

"No Sam, leave them alone. I swear I will never see Eugene again."

"That's what you said last time."

"I promise, I'll do anything if you leave them out of this."

"Anything?" Sam asked with a devilish smile. Cookie regretfully lowered her head and nodded.

"Don't worry, I'm not talking about that... At least not yet. How about you have dinner with me tonight? We can talk some more over a nice meal, and I have the perfect spot in mind."

"Ok Sam, whatever you say, just don't hurt them."

"Yeah alright, just be ready by 7:00pm." Sam gave her a sloppy kiss on the lips, and left as quickly as he had showed up.

*   *   *

Linda had been giving Eugene the silent treatment all day. He was trying to figure out what the problem was, but she continued to give him the cold shoulder. Eugene hoped that revealing that he had a surprise for her would change her mood.

"Baby, I know you've been down all day, and I really don't know why, but I have a little something planned for us tonight. It should brighten up your spirts." Eugene said smoothly. Linda decided to test the waters before she jumped in the pool.

"I woke up in the middle of the night and you weren't in bed. I looked outside and your car wasn't here either. I tried to call you, but you conveniently left your phone here. So where did you go?" Eugene's heart fell to his stomach. His wife was a lawyer, so he had to think fast and come up with something good.

"I couldn't sleep last night. I had to clear my head, so I took a ride. When I finally stopped for gas, I locked my keys in the car. I called Pop-a-Lock, but since it was so late, they took forever to come unlock it." He said retrieving the Pop-a-Lock receipt from his jogging pants pocket. Linda looked at the receipt. The time and date matched up, but her being the lawyer she was, Linda had to dig deeper.

"What had you so upset, that you had to take a ride in the middle of the night?" She asked, waiting on him to blame it on her like usual.

Linda thought he was going to say he had to clear his head because she accused him of knowing Miss Taylor. She was waiting for it, but he surprised her with his response.

"Baby I wasn't totally honest with you yesterday. See I do know Miss Taylor, well I used to know her. I didn't know how to tell you, but while I was riding around last night I realized that I don't want to lose you. Miss Taylor was a thing of my past... You are my now and forever." Eugene said looking in his wife's eyes.

He loved Cookie, but he couldn't offer her what she wanted. Eugene loved his family and he wasn't willing to give them up for anything. When he left Cookie's house, he had decided, that it would be the last time he saw her.

Linda wanted to believe him, her heart needed to believe, but her mind told her to pack her bags and leave him.

Maybe he is telling the truth. I'll see what he has in store tonight and just take it from there, she thought to herself.

*   *   *

"How did you manage to get a table in a spot like this?" Cookie asked Sam.

"Let's just say I know somebody, who knows somebody."

"If you say so... Why won't you tell me exactly what it is that you do for a living? Because you've only been home from prison for a few months, and you're driving a brand new Lincoln Navigator, bringing me to expensive restaurants and buying me all sorts of gifts. So what's the deal?"

"Well, if you really want to know, while I was in jail, I took medicine for my bipolar disorder, but for an entire year they were giving me the wrong kind of medicine. I got real sick and almost died. When my sister found out, she sued the prison. About two months before I was released I got a settlement check for 300 thousand dollars. So needless to say I'm working with a little something... I'm not holding like you are, but I'm doing okay." Sam joked.

"Ok... I hear that... Well since you're being all open and honest, won't you tell me how you always seem to know my business? You know who has been at my house, you got names, times, and dates. What's up with that?"

"What can I say, baby. I'm Psycho Sam." He laughed.

*　　*　　*

Linda was shocked as they pulled up to the valet in front of 'Mi Casa's'. It was a well-known restaurant, popular for its international dishes and high prices. The atmosphere was warm, the waiters were pleasant, and the food was to die for. Each booth was sectioned off and equipped with its own fire place.

When Linda walked in, the Maître' D handed her a single rose and escorted them to their reserved table. Linda looked at Eugene and kissed him deeply. They sat down on the butter soft cushions, and stared into each other's eyes. At that moment, Eugene knew that Linda was the one for him. Her anger was starting to subside, and he began to melt. They shared a nice conversation over a bottle of wine and dinner by the fire place. Everything was going well, until Eugene saw someone that looked like Cookie walk by his and Linda's booth. His whole demeanor changed instantly.

"What's wrong honey?" Linda asked, noticing the blank look on his face.

"Oh nothing, my stomach is feeling a little queasy, that's all."

"If you want we can skip dessert and go home. Besides, I have dessert waiting for you when we get there." Linda said with a seductive smile.

They finished their meal with light conversation, because Eugene's mind was on Cookie.

I wonder if that was really her, and if so, who she is here with. It doesn't matter, because I can't deal with her anymore, but she's like a drug and my family is rehab. I'm cool until I get near her, then I relapse. I don't know if its love or lust, but there's something about Cookie that I just can't get enough of, Eugene thought to himself.

After dinner, Eugene paid for their meals and they went to go wait while valet got their car. Eugene started checking his pockets like he was looking for something.

"Wait here honey. I left my credit card inside. I'm sorry, I'll be right back." Eugene said as he walked back inside the restaurant.

The place was dimly lit, and he was having a hard time trying to see who was here as he went from booth to booth, looking for Cookie, or the lady who looked like her. He just had to see for himself. Eugene finally found who he was looking for. She was sitting in a booth alone. Eugene got butterflies in his stomach as he approached her.

"Hey, Miss Taylor," he said casually. She spit out the wine she was sipping when she saw Eugene.

"What are you doing here?" She asked.

"I should be asking you the same thing. You're here all dressed up, looking good enough to eat. Are you here with someone?" Before she could answer,

Eugene heard a familiar voice behind him.

"Yeah, she's with me. Mr. Robinson. Do you have a problem with that?" Eugene turned around with a scowl on his face. He knew that voice belonged to none other than his crazy little cousin.

"Well, well if it ain't Crazy Sam. They finally let you out the Looney Bin." Eugene said, sarcastically. "You're damn right they let me out, and my name isn't Crazy Sam anymore... They call me Psycho Sam." Eugene laughed in his face and turned his attention back to Cookie.

"So Miss Taylor, when did you start hanging out with basket cases?" He asked. Cookie sat there speechless with a shocked look on her face.

"You two know each other?" She asked incredulously.o

"Yeah, he's my little cousin. But the question is how do you know him?"

"He's the ex-boyfriend I was telling you about." Eugene's mouth hit the floor as Sam slid in the booth next to Cookie.

"So I guess that us making love last night didn't mean anything to you then," Eugene said to Cookie, saying it only to piss Sam off.

"I guess not, because you went home to your wife afterwards." Cookie spat.

"But you know how I feel about you. I love--"

"That's enough buddy." Sam interrupted. "As you can see, we are trying to enjoy our dinner. So if you don't mind, won't you get lost? And word to the wise, stay away from Cookie or else."

"Or else what?" Eugene yelled, causing the other patrons to look around at them. "Silly Sam, Sorry Sam, Psycho Sam, or whatever you call yourself. You are the same little cousin I used to beat up back in the day, so unless you want to take a little trip down memory lane, I advise you to mind your business when I'm talking to my girl." Sam laughed loudly, but Cookie felt good to hear Eugene say that.

"Your girl? Did you forget that you're married? As a matter of fact, isn't that who you came here with? Where is your lovely wife, Linda?" Eugene had forgotten that Linda was waiting outside for him. He looked at Cookie and she didn't say anything. He wanted to say something, but he couldn't find the words. So he turned around and left, but not before making a promise to check Sam about trying to play him in front of Cookie.

*   *   *

"What took you so long?" Linda asked, waiting in the car.

"I ran into my cousin Sam."

"Wait... You mean the crazy one? I thought you didn't like him."

"I really don't care for him too much, but we haven't seen each other in over 5 years. We made plans to get together sometime real soon." He said with a sinister smile.

CHAPTER 13

Cookie was in another world as they rode back to her house. Sam noticed her silence, but he didn't know what to say without upsetting her even more.

"What's the matter?" He asked carefully. Cookie looked over at him with daggers in her eyes.

"Why didn't you tell me that you knew Eugene?"

"Does it matter if I know him or not? Would you have stopped sleeping with him, if I told you he was my cousin? NO. That's why I didn't tell you, because it wouldn't have made a difference."

"So, what I still have the right to know. And you tried to get over on me, by saying you would kill his family, if I didn't leave him alone." Cookie said.

"Oh, you thought I was joking when I said that? I'm dead serious, and I'll show you how serious I am if I catch y'all together again. I don't care anything about him, or his perfect little family." Cookie shook her head, but kept her mouth shut until she got home. Cookie got out of his car without saying anything to him. As she opened the front door, Sam rushed in behind her.

"What are you doing? I didn't invite you in. As a matter of fact, I don't want to even see you anymore, and if I catch you sneaking around here again, I swear I'll call the police on you." Cookie screamed into his face. It seemed like Sam's eyes changed right in front of her, as he quickly grabbed her throat.

"Who do you think you talking to like that? I spent 5 years in jail for you, and now you want to diss me?" Sam said through gritted teeth. Cookie clawed at the hand that was gripped tightly around her neck. Sam noticed her face changing colors due to lack of air, so he let her go.

"See how you've ruined a good night. We were supposed to come back here and make love until the sun came up." Sam said.

"I... Wouldn't... Have sex... With you... If you were ... The last man on earth." Cookie wheezed, trying to catch her breath. Sam smiled at her feistiness.

"You always were a fighter, just like Carol. She fought me to the very end. She even left me with a little souvenir." He said pointing to a bite mark on his finger, and the scratch on his face. Cookie's heart skipped a beat as she realized that Sam was the one who killed Carol, and she might be next.

"Please don't hurt me." She begged.

"I love you. I wouldn't hurt you... Of course, unless I couldn't have you, then I would make sure nobody had you." Cookie started crying as Sam slowly peeled the clothes off of her shaking body. He kissed her tears as he roughly thrust inside of her. She winced in pain as he continued to ram her dry sex.

*   *   *

Cookie sat down in the tub with the shower on. The water was as hot as it could go. She cried quietly while Sam sat on the toilet seat, lost in his own thoughts.

I really don't want to kill her, but she knows too much, and I'm not going back to jail. I should have never told her about Carol. Anyway, Cookie can't say that I raped her, because she didn't tell me to stop, besides I know she wanted it... The only question is, can I trust her?

"Cookie let me ask you something. Can I trust you not to go to the police?" He asked. Cookie didn't respond, she was deep in her own thoughts as well.

What am I gonna do? He's not gonna let me live if he thinks I'll turn him in. I can't believe that he had the nerve to rape me. I have to do something, but what... I know, I'll call Eugene and have him come over. I just have to play like everything is all good, until I can get to my phone. Her thoughts were interrupted when Sam snatched the shower curtain open.

"Don't you hear me talking to you?" He yelled.

"I'm sorry, baby, I was deep in thought. I didn't hear you." She said softly. The innocence in her voice calmed the beast within him.

"What were you thinking about?" He asked.

"I was thinking about us, and wondering if it could work. I mean what can we do different now, that we didn't do 5 years ago. I love you, I'm just afraid that you'll hurt me. Your jealousy could possibly be the death of me." She said on the brink of crying.

At that moment, Sam's stone cold heart began to melt. He stepped into the shower fully clothed, sneakers and all, and hugged her tight. Cookie smiled slightly as she realized she had him, hook, line, and sinker.

"Give me those wet clothes," Cookie said after getting dressed. Sam took off his clothes and she gave him a robe to put on. Cookie started laughing because the pink robe she gave him was too small. Sam looked in the mirror and laughed also. Cookie took the wet clothes down to the dryer in the basement, but not before snatching her cell phone off the nightstand.

She quickly threw the clothes in the dryer, turned it on and pulled out her cell phone. Her first thoughts were to call the police, but she wanted Sam to suffer for raping her. So she decided to stick with the plan and call Eugene. She wanted to call him, but Cookie figured that he was with his wife, so she sent him a text message instead:

'I know you probably don't want anything to do with me right now, but I really need your help!! Same is at my house and he won't leave. He raped me and said he'll kill me like he did Carol. Please help me. I need you... Cookie'

As soon as she sent the message, Cookie looked up and locked eyes with Sam, who was walking down the steps. She cursed herself, because the dryer was loud, and she didn't hear him open the basement door.

"What the hell are you doing?" He demanded.

"I-I was just checking my voice mail." She stammered.

Sam snatched the phone out of her hand and browsed through it. Satisfied that the last incoming call was from him, and the last outgoing call was made before they went to dinner, he stuffed the phone in his robe pocket. Then he grabbed her hand and dragged her up the stairs.

*   *   *

Eugene had just received the best oral sex this wife had ever given him. Feeling a little better after his encounter with Cookie and Sam, he went to the bathroom, and took a shower. Linda was on the phone with her son, Tommy. He and his sister, Gina, were spending the night with their grandparents. Eugene wanted the night for just him and his wife, so he had asked his parents to babysit the children, to which they happily agreed. While Linda was talking to Tommy, Eugene's cell phone vibrated 3 times. She looked towards the bathroom, and he was still in there. Linda could hear the water running and him singing along to a James Brown song. She quickly hung up with her son as curiosity got the best of her. Linda picked up his cell phone and tip toed to the bathroom. She opened the door and peeked inside. Linda smiled as she saw her husband singing and dancing to the music.

She thought about putting his phone back down, until she saw the words Text Message Received. As badly as she wanted to trust her husband, his past affairs made it hard for her to do that. So she checked the message and became instantly upset when she read it and saw that it was from Cookie.

Eugene walked out of the bathroom whistling, but stopped short, when he seen his wife sitting on the bed crying.

 "Baby what's wrong?" He asked bending down on one knee, and holding her hand. Linda smacked his face and pushed him away. Eugene stood up, holding his cheek with the shocked look.

 "What the hell is this?" She yelled, throwing the phone at him. Eugene was still confused, he picked up the phone and read the text message that Cookie had sent him. He immediately started getting dressed.

"Where are you going?" Linda asked through loud sobs.

"You read the message didn't you? I have to go help her. Ain't no telling what my crazy ass cousin will do."

"So you're gonna leave me just like that?"

"Baby, you are more than welcome to come with me. If you were in her position, wouldn't you want somebody to help you too?" Eugene said. Linda took a few seconds to respond.

"Before you go, let me ask you a question... When we were at the restaurant tonight, and you went back inside to get your credit card, was Cookie in there with Sam? And did you use the credit card thing as an excuse to go see her?"

Eugene remained quiet and from his silence, Linda already knew the answer.

He turned to leave and Linda called out to him.

"Why don't you just call the police for her and let them handle it." Once again, Eugene didn't say anything.

"If you walk out that door, I'm leaving you. And this time it will be for good. I'm taking the kids and we are gone." Linda cried.

"I'm sorry." Was all he said as he walked out of the room.

Eugene's mind was made up. He had to go and help her. He knew what Sam was capable of. Eugene felt like he would never be able to live with himself if something happened to Cookie, and he hadn't done everything he could to help. Eugene knew he was taking the risk of losing his family. But he thought after a few days, once Linda had calmed down, she would realize that he had done the right thing by going to Cookie's aid.

He went to the room that he had converted into an office. He removed the picture of Martin Luther King Jr, and behind it held a wall safe. He punched in the combination, opened it up and pulled out a shiny .32. He checked it for bullets, and put it in his pocket.

Eugene thought about going back to his bedroom, and explaining to Linda why he had to do what he was doing. But he thought it would be a waste of time. He said a short prayer, and kissed a family picture of him, Linda, and the kids, before quietly leaving.

When Eugene pulled up to Cookie's house, his stomach started doing back flips. He walked to the front door and could hear arguing. Sam was upset and on edge. He knew Cookie was up to something, but she kept denying that she had done anything wrong.

 "I swear Cookie, if you're tryna be slick, I'm gonna put you out your misery." Sam warned.

"Just like you did to my best friend?" Cookie said sarcastically.

"Yeah, just like I did Carol. You should have seen her face when I had my hands wrapped around her throat. It was pure magic."

"You sick bastard! Why did you kill her? What did she ever do to you?"

"She got in my way, by trying to keep you away from me. So she had to go. I heard her, kicking dirt on my name, while y'all were in the kitchen talking. It's called process of elimination. Your boy Tony woulda been next, but he quickly realized that you weren't worth dying over."

Cookie's emotions got the best of her.

"I. HATE. YOU!" She screamed. "I hate you with every ounce of blood in my body. You psychotic maniac. I wish you would just drop dead."

"You want me dead? Okay, but you first." Sam said, smacking her in the face. Cookie stumbled back and picked up a flower vase. She hurled it at him, but she missed and it smashed against the wall. Sam went to lunge at Cookie, but a knock at the door, stopped him.

He looked at Cookie, then he looked at the door and back at Cookie again. For the first time since being released from jail, Sam started to panic at the thought of going back to prison. His first instinct was to run out the back door, and that was what he was about to do, until he heard another knock, and Eugene's voice calling for Cookie. A sadistic smile crawled across Sam's face as he opened the front door.

CHAPTER 14

Eugene put his ear to the door and heard the arguing, but he couldn't make out what was being said, until he heard Cookie scream 'I Hate You'. A few moments later, he heard glass shattering against a wall. That's when he knocked on the door. Eugene got no answer, so he knocked again and called Cookies name.

"Cookie... Cookie open up. It's me, Eugene." He yelled, banging on the door. A few seconds later, Sam snatched the door open.

"Hey cousin, glad you could make it to the party. Come on in." Sam said smiling nastily. Eugene brushed passed Sam and rushed to Cookie's side.

"Hey baby. Are you ok?" He asked hugging her. Cookie broke down crying in his arms.

"Aww, that is so sweet. If this ain't a Kodak moment. Where's a camera when you need one?" Sam said clapping his hands.

"I came over as soon as I got your message. Did he hurt you?" Eugene asked.

"Oh, so you called him over here to save you. Well who's going to save him?" Sam said walking towards them.

Eugene pushed Cookie behind him and stepped toward Sam. No words were needed; they let their fists do the talking. Sam took the first swing. He threw a right hook, but Eugene side stepped it, and hit Sam with a crunching blow to the stomach. Sam was much bigger, due to his vigorous work outs, but Eugene was more experienced.

He hit Sam with a left hook that almost broke his cheek bone. Then Eugene landed a right elbow that took Sam down to one knee. Eugene moved in for the kill, but Sam caught him off guard with a nut crunching blow. Eugene fell to the ground in the fetal position, holding himself.

"I'm not the same little cousin that you used to beat up on." Sam said, standing up wiping the blood from his mouth. "Look at you now. All over some cookies that weren't even yours. You have a beautiful wife at home, but yet you want to be under my girl." Sam started kicking Eugene while taunting him with every blow.

"Next... Time... Stay... At Home... With... Ya wife." Sam paused to look up at Cookie, who was screaming for him to stop. That slight pause was all Eugene needed to turn the tables. He pulled the .32 from his pocket and aimed it at his cousin. Sam saw it out the corner of his eye and kicked it out of Eugene's hand just in time. The gun went off before it slid across the room.

"Damn family, you was really gonna shoot me? And they call *me* the crazy one." Sam said, as he continued to kick Eugene while he was still on the ground.

Cookie's next door neighbor heard the gun shots and called the police.

Sam had the look of death in his eyes. He started choking Eugene. Sam had beaten him up so badly that Eugene couldn't even fight back. Cookie was scared. Eugene's eyes were rolling in the back of his head, and she knew that if he died, then she would be next. That was not part of her plan. She didn't mean for anything to happen to Eugene. Out of fear and desperation, she picked up the gun off the floor. Her hands shook as she aimed the gun at the back of Sam's head.

 "Get off of him!" She yelled. Sam ignored her. "Don't make me shoot you." Cookie said with more force. That got his attention. Sam turned around and saw Cookie holding the gun. He smiled as he noticed her hands shaking. He knew she didn't have the guts to shoot him, so he went back to choking Eugene.

Cookie closed her eyes and fired the gun, letting off the remaining 5 shots. The first two missed their intended target.

The next two hit Sam In the side of his neck and his lower back. The last shot grazed his head. Cookie kept squeezing the trigger, well after the gun was emptied. Sam grabbed the side of his neck as blood squirted out like a water fountain. He fell forward and landed on Eugene. Cookie dropped the gun and fell to her knees, as she cried uncontrollably. Eugene pushed Sam off of him and went to Cookie's side. He held her in his arms and rocked her.

"I'm sure someone heard the gun shots, so the cops are probably on their way here. We have to get our story straight now." He whispered in her ear. Cookie nodded her head and wiped the tears from her face. "When the police get here, this is what we tell them. I shot Sam in self-defense. He beat and raped you. I came here to help, me and him got into a fight. He pulled the gun on me, we wrestled over it, and I shot him in self-defense... Okay?"

"But what if--"

"What if nothing, that's our story and we are sticking to it." Eugene said cutting her off. They filled in the gaps on their story and he wiped Cookie's prints off the gun.

Moments later, the police were storming into the house. They questioned a bloodied and bruised Eugene. They also interviewed Cookie, but she was so shaken up that they couldn't get much out of her. The paramedics took Sam to the hospital, but he died in the ambulance on the way there. Eugene was taken to the police station for more questioning. After hours of intense interrogation, Eugene slipped up and changed a few minor details in his story. Sam died as a result of too much blood loss, due to the being shot in the neck.

*   *   *

Eugene was eventually charged with second degree murder. The detective that was assigned to the case believed that Cookie was the one who had shot and killed Sam, but he had no proof. Eugene was taking the blame and Cookie was playing the victim, so he had no choice but to charge Eugene even though his gut told him that Miss Taylor was the one who had pulled the trigger.

After a long wait, Eugene finally got a chance to make a phone call. He called his wife at home so she could work on getting him out. The phone rang 4 times before the answering machine picked up. He left a message.

"Hi Linda baby, it's me. I'm in jail right now. I know I messed up, but me and Sam got into it and I shot him in self-defense. I'm being charged with murder and I need you to come bail me out. Since it's a weekend I have to wait until Monday to see a judge. I am in need of a lawyer, so see if someone from your law firm can represent me... Please... I know you're mad with me right now and I'm sorry, but baby I need you." He tried to call her cell phone next, but the police officer wouldn't let him.

*   *   *

Eugene sat in the holding cell and thought about how his life had turned from sugar to shit, ever since he met Cookie. Before Miss Taylor entered the picture, he and his wife were on good terms, his kids were healthy and he was working at a great job that he loved. Eugene felt like he was on top of the world... Now he was sitting in a jail cell, facing murder charges... All over some good Cookies.

*   *   *

Linda went to her sister's house, the night Eugene left. She spent the entire weekend there while her kids stayed with their grandparents. A weekend of rest and relaxation was just what she needed.

Linda decided to take Monday off so she could take care of the divorce papers. Her mind was made up; she had to let Eugene go. He had made his choice, when he left her alone to go and rescue another woman. Linda understood that Cookie needed help, if she was in the company of Crazy Sam, but Linda didn't know why Eugene didn't just call the police and let them take care of it.

Linda got home around noon. Just in time for the afternoon news. She threw her purse on the couch and turned on the TV. She checked the answering machine and saw that there were a few messages. The first one was from Eugene.

"Hi Linda baby, it's me--" was all she heard of the message before she erased it. Linda was in the middle of listening to a message left by a coworker, when she saw a mug shot of Eugene on the television. She put the phone down and turned up the TV.

"Eugene Robinson was charged with the murder of his cousin Samuel Nesmith. Witness' say the two cousins had a dispute over a mutual friend by the name of Natasha Taylor. She is also being questioned about the murder. Mr. Robinson claims the murder was an act of self-defense, but he is still being held without bail. Now in other news--"

Linda turned off the TV and broke into tears. She wanted to help her husband, but part of her wanted him to suffer.

Linda was embarrassed that Eugene would do something so crazy and risk his life and family. At that point, she decided that enough was enough, and that Eugene was on his own. She and the kids would move on.

CHAPTER 15

It took 3 months for Eugene's case to go to court. The whole time he was locked up, Cookie had not been allowed to visit him. She was cleared of all charges, but was issued a no contact order with him until after sentencing, but she sent him letters in Carol's name and that was how they kept in touch.

*   *   *

At Eugene's first case review, the prosecutor offered him a plea bargain of 15 years, but he didn't accept it. The lawyer Cookie got for him wanted Eugene to wait for a better deal.

After another four months and two more plea deals, came the day of his trial. They offered him 7 years to plead to manslaughter. His lawyer advised him to sign the plea, but Eugene wanted to take it to trial. He felt like if he stuck to the self-defense story, then he could beat the case, and possibly face no jail time at all. Eugene entered the courtroom with a black on black Armani suit, with snake skin shoes. It was the first time Cookie had seen him in 7 months. A single tear slowly crawled down her cheek, as she thought about Eugene doing time for a crime she committed. The trial went on for 2 days.

Cookie was called to the stand as a witness for the defense, but under cross examination, the prosecutor found loop holes in her testimony. The main thing that sealed Eugene's fate was the argument of Sam being shot in the back.

"How can you call it self-defense, if the victim was shot from behind?" The prosecutor repeated over & over.

Eugene was found guilty and sentenced to 20 years. A few weeks after the trial, Cookie was finally allowed to visit Eugene. She felt nervous as she sat on the stool waiting for Eugene to enter the visiting area. His eyes lit up and huge smiles spread across both of their faces when they saw each other. He cursed under his breath because they had to talk on the phone with a 6 inch plate glass window in between them, but still he eagerly picked up the phone.

"How are you doing, baby?" He said with a smile. Just his smile alone made her feel better.

"I'm ok, but I miss you like crazy," she replied. They talked for a while, until Cookie became silent.

"What's wrong?" Eugene asked. Cookie took a deep breath and stood up. Eugene's mouth hit the floor when he saw her pregnant belly.

"I'm 7 &1/2 months pregnant. We're gonna have a little boy." Cookie said rubbing her stomach. Eugene lowered his head in disappointment.

"What's the matter, baby? You don't have to worry about it. I have more than enough money to raise our son until you come home... I already told you that I'm not going anywhere. We are gonna ride this out together, all three of us... Besides, after your appeal or modification is granted, you could be out a lot sooner than we think."

Eugene didn't he respond. He closed his eyes and shook his head.

"Please don't be upset with me. The only reason I didn't tell you about the pregnancy is because I didn't want you to stress even more." Eugene opened his eyes and spoke so softly, she could barely hear him.

"Cookie, have you ever wondered why my son Tommy has a different last name then me?" Cookie nodded her head, trying to figure out where he was going with this.

"Well, it's because he's not my biological child. He has his birth father's last name. He's my step son. Tommy was 2 years old and Linda was almost 2 months pregnant with Gina when we met each other. Her ex-boyfriend was very abusive, so she left him. We met at my bank. I was the head teller back then, and she needed help with getting a loan. Anyway, we hit it off and dated for a few weeks before she told me she was 2 months pregnant. We ended up getting married before she gave birth. Even though the baby wasn't mine, she still named Gina after me. See, one of the reasons I was so excited and quick to marry Linda was because she was already pregnant when we met... The truth of the matter is, I was born with a rare prostate disease, which doesn't allow me to have kids of my own. So I thought Linda already being pregnant was heaven sent... Basically what I'm tryna tell you is, I can't have kids... So the baby that's growing inside of you right now isn't mine."

Cookie dropped the phone and started crying. She slid off the stool and onto the floor as the reality set in that she was carrying Psycho Sam's baby.

Eugene stood up and walked away with tears in his eyes. He'd lost his job, his family, and his freedom...

All for the love of GOOD COOKIES!

THE END